Michael woke up with a jump. He had been dreaming about a Spanish galleon laden with treasure, and he had been just about to lift the lid off a giant trunk when a sword flashed above him.

So begins *The Santa Maria*, a real adventure story.

A Hebridean boy lives with his grandfather. All his life he has heard whispers of a Spanish galleon that is supposed to have gone down off the island's coast with its promised treasure.

The story culminates in a great storm, and the hunt for *The Santa Maria* begins in earnest.

Aimed at 8–12 year olds, *The Santa Maria* gives readers a real sense of what living on an island is like. It deals also with issues of bullying, but most of all imparts a sense of adventure.

THE *Santa Maria*

KENNETH STEVEN

ARGYLL✤PUBLISHING

First published 2007
Reprinted 2008
Argyll Publishing
Glendaruel
Argyll PA22 3AE
Scotland
www.argyllpublishing.com

British Library Cataloguing-in-Publication Data.
A catalogue record for this book is available from the British Library.

ISBN 978 1 906134 02 0

Cover Art & Illustrations
Louise Ho

Printing
Atheneum Press, Gateshead

THE *Santa Maria*

KENNETH STEVEN

ARGYLL ✠ PUBLISHING

© Kenneth Steven 2007

First published 2007
Reprinted 2008
Argyll Publishing
Glendaruel
Argyll PA22 3AE
Scotland
www.argyllpublishing.com

The author has asserted his moral rights.

**British Library Cataloguing-in-
Publication Data.
A catalogue record for this book is
available from the British Library.**

ISBN 978 1 906134 02 0

Cover Art & Illustrations
Louise Ho

Printing
Atheneum Press, Gateshead

This book is for three special island friends:
Joyce Watson on Iona
and Joan and Angus Macdorald on Skye

1

MICHAEL woke up with a jump. He had been dreaming about a Spanish galleon, laden with treasure, and he had been just about to lift the lid off a giant trunk when a sword flashed above him. The rain was pattering against his window like fingertips. The wind came in long gusts, knocking against the chimney and the roof slates. It was Monday morning and it was twenty past seven.

He always knew exactly what time it was the moment he woke up. It was the strangest thing, but it had always been that way. Many's the time it had saved him when his alarm had let him down. He huddled under the warm blankets, his eyes still sleepy.

The door of his room creaked. He listened. Someone was there.

'Boy!' The loud whisper of his grandfather. He stuck his head out from the blankets.

'I'll be there soon,' he whimpered.

'Eight minutes and forty-two seconds!' his grandfather told him.

The whole room was rattling with the wind. He pulled back the curtains and everything he saw was grey – the sea, the sky, the shore. Puffin Billy, the postman, was coming down the road in a wiggly line, either because he had been drinking too much again, or because he had a heavy parcel for somebody.

The road was shining with rain. It was in deep grey puddles, and they all rippled when the wind blew through. Michael wished suddenly that it might be possible to be rained in. After all, it was possible to be snowed in, so why not rained in? Then school might be closed for days and days on end each winter. . . A tapping woke him from his thoughts. It was his grandfather poking the living room ceiling down below with his stick. Michael began pulling on his clothes in the draughty little room. He had goose-bumps all over his arms and he dressed as quickly as he could. He yawned like a lion, splashed some water on his face, put a comb through his hair, then clattered downstairs and sat down in his chair in the living room.

'Eight minutes fifty seconds,' his grandfather told him accusingly.

'Did you have to go to school in the rain, grandpa?' Michael asked

His grandfather got up from his seat. 'Even if there was six feet of snow we had to go to school. The only excuses were death or bubonic plague.'

'What's bubonic plague?'

His grandfather plonked a big bowl of porridge down in front of him. 'If you eat that, you won't get it.'

The rain whistled down the chimney and banged against the slates. Michael shivered and began his porridge. Outside in the street, he saw George, Fergus and Ewan marching along, swinging their bags round their heads.

8

The old clock on the mantelpiece clacked away. There was going to be a maths test this morning – the thing Michael hated more than anything. He hunched over his porridge – what a start to the week.

'When you come home this evening, boy, you can take Jess for a walk.'

The collie's ears rose for a moment at the sound of her name, and the big black eyes followed the old man as he sat down at the table. He'd always called Michael boy; he didn't mean anything bad by it, in fact he meant it kindly. His own soft blue eyes watched the boy as he spooned in the last of the porridge. He would eat his own once Michael was gone. At twenty past eight Michael was ready at the door. He had an orange in his pocket. He called goodbye to his grandfather.

'Here, there's a letter to post.' His grandfather came out to the porch with a big envelope and handed it to him. He frowned.

'Is there anything wrong, boy?'

'No, I'm fine, just in a hurry. I'll post the letter.'

Then he was gone into the rain. It was wild outside and he set off running at once. He could hear Jenny Mackay calling behind him, but he pretended he hadn't heard and ran on. The mist was rolling over the island like cotton wool; it was hardly higher than the roofs in the village street. There was no-one else about except kids on their way to school, some of them looking like drowned rats already. At the church gate he stopped and looked about him. There wasn't a soul – Jenny hadn't turned the corner

9

yet. He slipped through the iron gate and hid beside the little shed against the wall where Colin, the gardener, kept his tools. He wouldn't be about today.

He was dry there, and out of the worst of the wind. At last he heard the church bell, ringing out nine heavy times. His heart raced a bit faster. He'd never done this before, not in his whole life. He could hear Miss MacLennan in his mind getting up in front of the class.

'Right, all of you, I hope you've been working hard on your maths over the weekend. You have an hour to do these questions and not a minute longer. It's important for each and every one of you. . .'

Michael went through the church grounds and into the little lane at the back. It was very important that no-one should see him – everyone knew everyone else on the island. But there wasn't a soul about. He hid his bag at the back of a den he and Fergus had worked on over the summer. He made sure it would stay dry however hard it rained. Then he began running. He ran up the track that led away to the north end of the island. The wind was like the paw of a lion, batting against him and playing with him. But the skies were clearing to the north, and that thrilled Michael's heart. He was going to his favourite place on earth. Now he was out of the worst danger. There were only a couple of farms to pass on the way, and he'd keep low, under the stone wall along the side of the track. Suddenly he felt excited, a joy went through his heart and he laughed aloud. He'd escaped school for the first time in his life and he didn't feel guilty – he felt good! He looked up at the grey skies and laughed with glee. He'd got away with it, that was the best thing of all.

By the time he got to the north end he could see blue sky over the islands to the north – Reneval and Skarva. The wind was dying a bit too, he was sure of it. Down below him was a wide sweep of grey sand. You could see where the tide had come up on different days; there were streaks of seaweed and shells. Over on the far edge, to Michael's left, was a great stone hill that stuck out like a Viking's nose into the sea. It was the tallest point of the island, and it was made of jet black rock. Michael always felt odd there; he could never quite understand why, but it was as if the rock were hiding some great secret. He was drawn back and back to it time and again, but he never knew if it was just his imagination. He went running down onto the shore to the other side of the beach, the right hand edge. That was the corner where the pebbles were, between great guardian boulders that looked like hunched old giants. You could find green stones there; strange little things that were see-through, the colour of lemon or lime. Somewhere out off the island there was a great rock of it, and the waves kept on breaking off tiny pieces and polishing them until they were done.

Old Morag who lived on the other side of the island with her cat MacTavish had told him another story. Once, a very long time ago, there had been a monastery on the island. One day one of the monks was out walking at the north end when he saw a beautiful creature swimming at the edge of the tide. It was a mermaid. The monk and the mermaid talked together for many hours and they fell in love. Already that day they decided to marry. But when the monk went back to the monastery to ask for permission he was told he could never marry someone from the sea. And when the mermaid swam back to the deep sea and asked to be allowed to marry the monk, she was told she could never marry someone from the land. Forever afterwards the mermaid sits by the rocks at the north end weeping, and her tears are little green stones. Of course that was just one of Old Maggie's stories – it wasn't really true. . .

Michael found one or two stones. Then a much bigger wave came right over his shoes and soaked the bottom of his trousers too. The chill of the water was like daggers. He felt cold and miserable. He had a long time to wait until school was done. He trailed over with his wet and heavy feet to the great mound of stone at the other side of the beach. Right out at the end of it was somewhere he had discovered a long time ago. It was hard to spot if you weren't looking for it. You could only go there at low tide, otherwise it was filled with seawater. There it was, a narrow black hole between the rocks. Michael knelt down in the dry sand and crawled inside, bent as low as possible so as not to hit his head on the stones that formed the roof. His head and shoulders disappeared, then his feet too. Inside, the passage opened into a cave, so tall he could stand upright. At the back he had a hidden store of sticks and paper, and one or two matches. He built a little wigwam of a fire once his eyes had grown used to the darkness;

then he struck his first match. It fizzled out. But the second lit an edge of paper and soon the sticks were crackling merrily. His eyes stung a bit with the smoke, but most of it drifted upwards and somehow found its way out of the cave. He had half his orange and wished he had some tea. He looked at his watch. Now the maths test would be over. He wondered what Miss MacLennan would say and shifted his feet awkwardly. He could hear his heart in his chest.

He imagined himself sitting at his own desk in the classroom. Miss MacLennan was writing at her big desk, her head bent over her paper. There wasn't a sound in the room. And Michael was looking at the girl who sat in front of him, Maria. Her long dark gold hair reached down her back in swirling curves. He loved it particularly when she shook those curls; they spilled round her shoulders like wild snakes. He looked into the fire and thought about her now. She was so different from all the other island girls. Most of them were dark and small; their hair was black, sometimes frizzy. Maria was different, and it wasn't just her hair that made her different. She didn't go about with the other girls at the weekend; she wasn't with them up at the village shop or down by the garage. She was off on her own, just wandering and exploring. Once Michael had seen her up at the north end, searching the edge of the tide for treasures, her hair billowing about her head. He'd thought about going down to talk to her, but then he felt silly and his heart pounded in his chest. He hid in the dunes until she had disappeared, and then he wished like mad that he'd had the courage to speak to her. There was something

lonely about her he liked. That was the thing that meant
more than anything else to him.

He took off his shoes and socks and dried them beside
the little dragon of fire. He warmed his feet till they were
hot and pink. He wished he'd brought a book with him,
although even with the fire there wasn't very much light
to read by. He listened to the waves booming against the
rocks outside and kept the fire alive by sacrificing his last
two bits of wood. In half an hour there would be no more
left.

He looked at the little pieces of green stone in the
firelight. When he held them up to the light they became

see-through and pale. But he wanted to find real treasure, something extraordinary. Perhaps the Vikings that came to the island to rob the monastery had left some of their treasures in the dunes. Perhaps the monks themselves had hidden something like the Book of Kells, a priceless thing that had been lost and buried for a thousand years. What if he were the one to find it? But where was there to look? Archaeologists had come to the island not long ago and dug over every corner of the ruined monastery. All they had found had been a few bones and some carved stones. How could he ever find anything more? The fire was beginning to fail and he dragged on his socks and shoes with a heavy heart. Already he was feeling the draught there – no point staying and getting a chill. He began to feel that perhaps it hadn't been such a good idea after all.

At ten to four he left the shelter of the shed beside the church and went out into the road. He had his bag back over his shoulder; none of his books had got even the slightest bit damp. It had been a long day. He'd been cold and hungry and fed up. It was something he wouldn't do again for a long time.

There was hardly any daylight left. The wind had got up again and the skies were wild and blue-black. He turned the corner and started off down to the house. He tried to feel normal but his heart was hammering in his chest. He didn't want to lie to his grandfather. The less he said about the day the better. He got to the front door and paused, his white hand on the knob of the door. He was rehearsing the things he'd say.

'Hello, that's me home,' he called, and went charging up the stairs the moment he came in.

'Right, come down when you are ready, boy. There's someone here I want you to meet.'

He threw his schoolbag onto his bed. What if it was Maria? What if she had come to see him? A thrill of hope filled his heart. He put a comb through his wet hair just in case and thumped downstairs, taking the steps two at a time. He burst into the living room.

He looked straight at her. Miss MacLennan was sitting in the other chair by the fire. It looked as if she had been eating sour apples, and her face was white as ash.

'Miss MacLennan says you weren't at school today, boy. She wants to know where you were when there was a maths test. And oh, by the way, you've still to walk the dog. I hope you won't mind getting a bit wet.'

2

ON SATURDAY afternoon Michael was bored. He had cleared out the fireplace for his grandfather and he had brought in fresh kindling and a bucket of coal. He had even done some homework for Miss MacLennan, although he hadn't forgiven her for coming to the house two evenings before. He had thought he would die.

It was a nothing sort of a day. The island was covered with a fishnet of mist and you couldn't see the mainland. There wasn't so much as a breath of wind, and that was a mighty unusual thing on Coolin. Nobody seemed to be about. Old Macaskill stood at the pier looking out to sea, his pipe letting out little tufts of smoke. Dawn, the big sheepdog from Alinish Farm, wandered about the grass at the top of the shore in search of interesting smells. The summer was over and there were no tourists crowding round the village shop, wanting postcards and souvenirs. It was just a normal day in autumn, and suddenly Michael realised that a long winter lay ahead of them. It would be like this until April the following Spring. He liked it when the tourists were gone because they didn't ask stupid questions or try to feed the sheep sweets, but now that they were gone it made the island very quiet indeed. He stood at the window in the living room misting the glass with his breath and drawing funny faces in the glass. The day was so long. . .

'Why don't you go and see Morag?' his grandfather suddenly asked, putting down his newspaper. 'You're like a boat without a sail today, boy, and Morag would do you good.' He picked up his newspaper again and the fire crackled in the grate.

Morag, he hadn't been to see Morag for ages, that was true. He stopped drawing with his finger and gazed through the window. For a moment he wasn't sure. He looked at the clock – five past three. He couldn't stay here waiting all day – he'd go mad.

'Take Morag those oranges,' his grandfather said, not looking up this time. It was as though he could read his thoughts sometimes. How had he known he had decided to go? 'Morag loves oranges more than anything in the world.'

Michael ran from the house and had his bicycle out of the shed in a moment. He jumped onto it and was away, the net of bright oranges swinging from his left hand. He realised in a moment they were the only thing of colour in the whole world that day – everything else, even himself, was grey.

Morag lived away over on the west side of the island. She had come to baby-sit in the days when his grandfather had to be away cutting peats or helping with lobsters. When he was really young Michael had believed she knew all the stories in the world. And she hadn't read them because she was blind – she'd heard them. There were as many stories in Morag's head as there were fish in the sea. Now he cycled quickly because he wanted to get there as fast as possible; he splashed through puddles and rang his bell at a wet huddle of sheep in the middle of the track. They moved reluctantly away, looking at him with big orange eyes like marbles.

He got to the top of the hill and had to stop for breath. The ferry was coming over from the mainland, appearing through the fur of mist. There would be hardly a soul on it, he thought. The ship was all lit up so it looked as though it was made of jewels. Now it was downhill almost the whole way to Morag's, to her farm at Claddich. This was the easy bit. He began bumping down the track, and now he could see someone moving in the farm kitchen window. He could imagine the smell of baking and the sound of MacTavish the cat's loud purring. In ten minutes he would be there again.

Except there was a pool he had to find a way of getting round, and he got one foot wet in a filthy puddle, so by the time he actually wheeled his way up to Claddich Farm he was tired and angry. There was Morag on the doorstep, wiping her hands on her apron.

'Michael MacGregor, fancy you coming here today.'

Michael stopped in his tracks. 'How did you know it was me?'

She laughed aloud. 'I may be blind, but I'm not stupid.' She waited until he'd left the bike against the wall, then whispered loudly, 'MacTavish tells me everything!' She burst into loud laughter and he went into the warmth of the hall, took off his muddy boots.

'And do I smell oranges?' she asked, frowning.

'Yes,' Michael said, handing her the net. 'A present from my grandfather. He knows you love them.'

She put her nose to the net. 'You know, Michael, I was four years old before I smelled an orange. I found a box of them washed up on Claddich Beach and I thought it was treasure. In a way it was. My mother shared those oranges with everyone on the island.'

He sat down in the big armchair by the fire and his feet didn't touch the ground. The rain pattered against the pane and he was glad he'd arrived in time. The farmhouse smelled of peat and butter, of MacTavish, of old carpet, of smoke, of exciting things.

'Did you ever hear of treasure on Coolin?' Michael asked. He tried to put the question normally, without sounding too excited, because she might laugh at him. But his heart raced all the same. She didn't answer at once. She sat in the armchair opposite him and MacTavish came slowly from the other side of the room and jumped up onto her knee. He could purr like a tiger. She scratched his ears and throat – there was nothing he loved better.

'Treasure on Coolin,' she said, her voice dreamy. 'Was there ever treasure on Coolin, MacTavish?' The old clock in the hall struck four and the rain became heavier. He stretched out to warm his hands. 'I've never told anyone this story before, Michael, so I hope you'll keep it safe. I think you will. My father was like you, he was always dreaming of treasure. He wanted the old stories about pirates to be true, that was all that was in his head. He would go out searching the beaches and the sand dunes all the months of the year when he should have been doing his lessons and working to get to college. Well, one of the old folk told him to look up at the north end. She said that in Gaelic the old name for the big hill was the Rock of the Spanish Galleon. He went up there searching after that, every minute he had, and one day he came back with something. D'you see that box on the mantelpiece?'

Michael nodded. Somehow he had lost his voice.

'Well, open it and tell me what's there.'

He got up and went over to the fireside. It wasn't a big box and it was roughly made. It was like nothing he had ever seen before. Very carefully he opened the lid. There, inside, was a cloth bag. It wasn't big, but whatever was inside was heavy all right. He lifted it and found the opening, poured whatever it was into his hand. It was a coin, bright and shining. Its edges weren't even and there was the head of a king on one side. He couldn't believe how heavy it was.

'That's a coin from the Spanish galleon,' Morag said. It was the only treasure my father ever found, and it came from up at the north end, from the hill.'

'But why the hill?' Michael said confused. 'How could the ship be in the hill? I don't understand.'

'Ah, there's the mystery,' Morag said, and she laughed again. When she laughed like that, she rocked backwards and forwards so all of her shook. She stroked MacTavish who had no answer either.

'That's a present for you,' she said quietly when she

could laugh no more. 'I know you'll treasure it as much as my father did. And perhaps you'll even be able to solve the mystery he puzzled over all his life.'

When Michael got home in the rain he could hear the television in the living room. His grandfather must be watching the news. He slumped down in a chair, his hair sticking up like the prickles of a hedgehog. His grandfather turned to look at him, his eyes twinkling.

'D'you think there was ever a Spanish galleon wrecked on Coolin?' he asked.

'No! I've told you not to believe a word that Morag tells you! She's a storyteller, boy, the best storyteller on the island. If Morag went to Hollywood, they'd listen to her stories for hours, writing them all down for films. Morag would come back a millionaire. But there's not one of her stories is true, boy, just you remember that. Now off with you to bed or you'll never be up in the morning!'

Michael didn't need to be told twice. He went upstairs to his bedroom and watched the moon rising over the sea like a golden coin. It lifted through the rain clouds and hung there like a single eye, watching him. Michael took out the heavy gold coin from his pocket. This was one story that had to be true.

He didn't close the curtains that night but lay for a long time watching the coin of the moon in the sky. About midnight he heard his grandfather tramping slowly up the stairs and switching off the upstairs light. The wind got up through the night and Michael dreamed he was out on a ship. There were ropes and tall masts all around him, and he could hear the sound of the waves. Then, all of a sudden, the face of Maria's was above his and he could hear her whispering strange words in a language he couldn't understand. She was holding a gold coin in her fingers.

3

'MICHAEL MacGREGOR, would you pay attention to the board and not to the seagulls in the street!' The class laughed loudly. Miss MacLennan walked up between the rows of desks and stood in front of his. They were all looking at him, smiling and laughing. His cheeks were on fire. He thought he might explode with embarrassment any moment. He tried to hide the piece of paper he had been scribbling on, but it was too late. She had eyes like a hawk – she missed nothing.

'What's that you've written there?' Miss MacLennan asked. She spoke loudly so all the class could hear and share his humiliation. He didn't know where to look, he didn't know what to do with himself. 'It's just something I wrote,' he muttered. She snatched it up from the desk, like a hen pecking a worm. Then she turned round to face the rest of the class and read aloud.

'Is there a Spanish galleon hidden up at the north end? Can there be more gold coins hidden in the rocks? What did Morag's father really find?'

The class roared with laughter, they rolled about in their seats and Jenny Mackay was almost crying with mirth. The walls were shaking. Michael sat hunched in his seat wishing he could disappear altogether. This was the worst moment of his life so far, and it seemed to go on for ever. The only person who hadn't turned round to mock him was Maria. He caught a glimpse of her long dark gold hair down her back – he didn't think she was laughing either.

Suddenly Miss MacLennan turned round again towards him, bent down and tapped the top of his head hard. 'Hello, is there anyone at home?' she said. 'Can anyone hear at all or have they all gone off looking for treasure at the north end of the island?' Now she wasn't amused any more, she was just angry. The rest of the class realised, and their loud laughter fell away until it was gone completely. 'Could Michael MacGregor please come back very quickly to the classroom and concentrate on his arithmetic, or else there's going to be trouble for a long time to come!'

She crumpled up the piece of paper into a tight ball, gave him a last angry glance, and marched back up towards the blackboard. She tossed the piece of paper into the air and it landed right in the bucket. 'Now we can get back to fractions.'

The afternoon dragged by. Michael didn't dare write another single word; he didn't even think about the Spanish galleon or the gold coin. But he found it hard to think about fractions either. He was still going over everything that had happened – the laughter, the way she'd read what he'd written aloud, the crumpling up of his bit of paper. She might as well have taken his heart and thrown it into the basket. He felt cold and raw all over. He felt sick. It was a Friday afternoon and normally he was full of anticipation, thinking about fifty different things he'd do over the weekend. But not that Friday. All he wanted was to get home as fast as he could and bury himself in his bedroom. He hated Miss MacLennan so much; she had made him feel as small as a rat.

She didn't ask him any questions. That was just as well too, because he couldn't concentrate properly on what she was saying. It was as if her voice was very far away, somehow he could only hear some of her words. He wouldn't have been able to answer any of her questions and she would just have shouted at him all the more.

At last the bell went for the end of the day. People were talking and laughing all round him; he could hear chairs being pushed under desks and the jostling of feet. He picked up his jotter and pens and got up. He crouched down on the floor slowly putting things away. He wanted to be the last to leave so that they couldn't laugh at him any more. Then he saw there was someone standing beside him, someone waiting for him. For a moment he was sure it would be Miss MacLennan and he felt a wave of fear pass through him. But it wasn't Miss MacLennan, it was Maria. She was looking at him shyly and the last of the class were leaving as Miss MacLennan rubbed out all the fractions on the board. 'Would you like to go to the north end? I usually go up there early in the morning. I thought you might like to.' She was holding all her books up to her chin and she looked away now as he looked at her.

'Yes, yes of course! OK!' His heart was thumping.

'All right, I'll come by the house just after seven.'

She was gone. He was the last to leave and if looks

could have killed, Miss MacLennan's would have given him a horrible death. But he didn't care, it didn't matter. He was so thrilled he ran the whole way home through the warm autumn rain. He was an athlete winning the hundred metres at the Olympics, winning the gold medal.

All through that long night he didn't sleep properly. It was like Christmas Eve, waiting for the present you know is downstairs waiting by the tree. It was a wild night outside; there was a branch tapping against the window that sounded like someone sending signals in Morse code. The wind came and went; sometimes it seemed to have died completely, but it was just holding its breath before rising again and bellowing round the houses of the island street. Once Michael went to the window and peered out. He caught a glimpse of a boat in the Sound, rocking its way north, all lit up and strange. He was glad he wasn't on it; he watched it until it vanished out of sight.

When he went back to bed he thought about Maria. He realised he didn't know much about her. She lived up at the top of the village in the manse, and her father was the church minister. But he didn't know anything about her mother at all, not the first thing. He tried to work out how that could be, because everyone knew everyone else on Coolin. He wished that he'd asked his grandfather, because anything he didn't know wasn't worth knowing, but it was too late now – he'd been in his bed for an hour and more. He wondered what he would talk to her about. School was boring, that was the last thing he wanted to bring up. But when he thought what else there might be he began to panic. What if she wasn't interested? What if he made a fool of himself?

But then he remembered that day in class and how she'd waited for him. She hadn't laughed at him like the rest of them. Maybe she really was different as he'd always believed her to be. He felt less afraid and he drifted into a light sleep. He was out in a ship, lying in a wooden cabin on board an old ship. He could hear the masts creaking and the sound of the waves; he could feel the ship lifting and falling beneath him. He didn't know why he was there but he knew he was on a strange and terrible voyage.

When he woke up next it was just beginning to get light and the rain was splintering against the window. It was just before six and the grey light was pale under the curtains. He remembered at once that Maria was coming to find him and he felt a stab of gladness that hurt his heart, but in a good way. He realised he mustn't forget to write a note for his grandpa telling him he'd gone up to the north end, and he staggered out of bed to find a stub of pencil and some paper.

Gone to the north end, he wrote and wondered if that was enough. He had nearly added with Maria, but he was glad he had decided not to. He got dressed and found that his hands were trembling. When he stopped to think why, he felt strange and dizzy.

He looked outside from the landing window and saw a sudden pool of light falling on the sea. A moment later it was gone. Blown away by the wind. Another gust came and rattled the window. He creaked down the wooden

staircase, pausing for a second outside his grandfather's room to hear his soft breathing. He made a cup of tea, a wonderful dark brown colour, just the way he liked it. Jess padded over and looked at him with big eyes, put her head against his hand.

'No, Jess, you can't come with me this time, girl. I promise I'll take you for a walk later.'

When he padded upstairs to his room a few minutes later, he heard a sudden rattling of stones against the window. It was five past seven and it was Maria – right on time. He went down to the porch, hearing his heart loud in his chest.

She giggled when she saw him.

'What's wrong?' he said, pulling the door behind him.

'Your hair – you look like a hedgehog!'

For a second he felt embarrassed, but she was just teasing, the way his grandfather often did. Her own gold

brown hair was tied in a knot at the back, and it made her look different.

'So, are we going to the north end?'

He nodded, his hands deep in his pockets.

'All right then, I'll race you. First one to the beach!'

They set off up the side lane that led between the houses. Maria was ahead of him, and there was no way he could have overtaken her, even if he'd wanted to. He almost slipped and fell on a patch of mud and she turned round, flashed a smile at him and went on again. This was the last thing in the world he'd expected. They ran on to the middle track he'd followed the other day when he didn't go to his maths test and now Maria really was flying. It was all he could do to keep up with her. He wanted to call to her, tell her to stop, but then she really might laugh at him. He had the beginnings of a stitch in his left side and his heart seemed huge as a house. Then the rain started from the west; it came in over the hills and ridges in a grey whirl and everything vanished. The mist covered it all like a great grey net. It was freezing rain, the left-hand side of his face felt so numb and cold. Still Maria kept running, and he thought he could hear her laughing now. Was she getting further ahead of him? When he was almost on the point of calling to her to tell her he was giving up, they broke over the sand dunes at the north end. Michael wasn't looking where he was going and his knees gave way beneath him. He tumbled down head over heels and lay on his back, covered in wet sand, gasping for breath. When he opened his eyes he saw Maria looking down at him, her hands on her hips. Now she was laughing at him.

'You're not very fit, Michael MacGregor, are you?'

He got up in the end and trailed after her, over to the other side of the beach with the great mound. She was dragging a stick behind her, singing something to herself. The tide was still quite far out – he decided he'd show her the cave.

'This is my secret,' he said, going down on his hands and knees to crawl inside the dark hole in the rocks. But once they were both inside she disappointed him.

'I've come here lots of times. When I want to get away from everything, at home or at school. I bring a notebook to write stories. I can escape in my imagination, pretend I'm somewhere far away.'

Michael was still thinking about secrets. All of a sudden he remembered he had another, hidden deep in his left pocket. He scrabbled to find it. The light was bad in the cave. He could just make out Maria's face, but everything

32

else was blurred and dark. He held the coin in the middle
of his palm and she gasped. Even though there was so
little light it shone like a sun.

'Where did you get that?' she whispered.

'From Morag, Morag over at Claddich. She told me her
Dad found it right here. It's Spanish, from one of the ships
of the Armada.'

Maria reached out her hand to touch the coin. He let
her hold it, glowing because this was a bigger secret by far
– one that really had meant something.

'Where did he find it?' she whispered, not looking at
him but at the coin.

'That's what I don't quite get. Morag says he found it on
the hill, the hill up above us. It doesn't make sense.'

Suddenly she looked at him and now he could see her all right, maybe because his eyes were getting used to the dim light. He could see the white oval of her face and the dark gold of her long hair. He thought she looked as if she had been washed on to the island from somewhere far away. He had to pinch himself to be sure he wasn't dreaming, that this really was happening.

'You know my dad?' she asked.

He nodded. Everyone on Coolin knew the minister, even the ones who didn't go to church on a Sunday.

'This is my secret,' she said, 'and you mustn't tell a single soul. But the story is that way, way back our family came from a Spanish ship, just like this coin. That we have Spanish blood in us.'

'Then maybe there really was a ship,' he said softly, thinking aloud and leaning his head back against the rock. Then suddenly he thought of something else and loudly blurted out his thought, 'Where's your Mum, Maria? Why do I never see her around?'

The second he had spoken the words he knew he should never have opened his mouth. She looked at him for a second and her eyes brimmed with tears, and then she was gone. He called her name and tried to hold her back but she'd gone. He scrabbled outside and saw her running for all she was worth over the beach; he was sure he could hear her crying.

'Maria!' he shouted, but the wind whipped his voice to shreds. Maria had gone.

4

ALL THAT LONG winter Michael missed Maria. At school her back was straight and hard. She didn't even shake her head to let her curls ripple on her back the way she used to, as if she'd known that was something special to him. It was the wettest autumn he could remember. Every day the rain seemed to be singing from the roofs and chimneys; every evening he came home like a drowned rat.

'No supper until you've dried that hair of yours, boy!' his grandfather told him, and Jess moved from beside the peat fire to let him crouch down to get dried.

Puffin Billy would call at the house every morning, his red oilskin shining with rain. He gave Michael a toothless grin and ruffled his hair.

'You'll be taking the boat to school again!' he laughed, and left most of the rain from his jacket in the porch.

Michael hoped against hope there might be a letter from Maria. He didn't really believe there would be, but there was a corner of him that still hoped all the same. When he woke up very early in the morning, knowing it wasn't more than twenty past six, listening to the crystals of rain against the window, he closed his eyes and that little corner of him believed that Maria would write to him. But every morning all the letters were for his grandfather as usual.

For a time he wanted to ask someone if they knew what had happened to Maria's mother. He nearly did one Sunday morning at breakfast when his grandfather was buttering some toast. The question was almost on the tip of his tongue when the old man scraped back his chair, remembering he had left a pot of porridge on the stove. After that the time never seemed right. He thought of going over to Claddich Bay to ask old Morag, but the days were so miserable he had little wish to get another soaking. And his grandfather was right; Morag was too good at telling stories. What she didn't know she often made up.

One day after games he almost asked Fergus. Fergus had red curls, often blushed, and could be very rude when he was with all the boys in the class at one time. But on his own he was fairly sensible and reliable, and often he knew things. He was kicking a stone along the road home and the island seemed completely asleep at four o'clock in the afternoon. Michael decided he would pluck up courage and ask him. Mrs Macdonald was pulling the living room curtains of Shuna Cottage. What if Fergus were to tell the others he had been asking about Maria? Perhaps they might make fun of him and that would make Maria hate him even more than she did now. Then Ewan's bicycle came jangling round the corner and he and Fergus were roaring with laughter about something to do with Miss MacLennan, and that was the moment lost. Michael went inside and banged the door and went up to his bedroom and lay there in the dark until supper.

One Sunday he even trudged up to the manse in the hope of seeing Maria. He didn't really know what he was going to do when he got there but he went all the same. It was just beginning to get dark and he hadn't much to do. His grandfather was watching television and it was all about politics – nothing made Michael more annoyed than political programmes. His grandfather had told him he needed to polish his shoes for school and Michael had said there was nothing wrong with them. In the end he was fed up and said he was going out. He banged the door and as he thumped upstairs he could hear his grandfather's muffled voice telling him to be back by twenty-five past six to set the table. He pulled on his coat and listened to the rain on the skylight window. Was it worth getting wet? Then he remembered Maria.

As soon as he went out he regretted it. His feet were wet from puddles before he reached the end of the village street. He ran from then on, uphill all the way, and by the time he was standing at the top of the manse track he was out of breath and his shoes were half full of rain. The lights were on in the house, in the living room. He went a bit closer, very quietly, hands deep in his pockets. Maria's father was in the kitchen, stirring a pan on the stove. He was speaking, and suddenly Maria appeared. Michael's heart lifted. Maybe she would look up and see him, notice him watching her out there in the pouring rain, and come out to call to him. He would be able to tell her he was sorry, that he'd never meant to hurt her, and everything would be all right. But he could see them, they couldn't see him.

And even if she had been able to, it was only a dream that she might ever forgive him.

He stood there a moment longer, thinking back to that morning when she'd come with him to the north end and he'd blurted out that question about her mother. Whatever had happened must have been awful or else she would never have been so upset. He looked inside the window and saw Maria's long dark hair glistening in the light. He had to find some way of saying sorry, he had to.

He thought about it the whole way home but could find no answer. The night was wetter than ever and little rivers were running down the street, glistening like snakes in the lights. Sometimes he wondered just how it was the island hadn't been washed away completely after all those years of rain. Just as he had his hand on the door handle he thought of it – he had to find treasure for Maria. The two of them were linked by the story of the Spanish galleon – it was the thing they had in common – so that was what it had to be.

As often as possible that winter he went up to the north end. Sometimes he took Jess with him for company and she chased ahead of him like a black and white waterfall. She was good company, even if she couldn't speak. He reckoned she understood a good deal of what he said to her; she looked at him with her big, wise eyes and seemed to know what he was thinking. The only time that he and Jess fell out was when she rolled in something dead, then the only one who thought Jess was intelligent was Jess herself.

Michael's birthday came at the end of November. It was the very darkest time on the island. Often the wind rattled the walls and the windows all day long. There was a chart marking all their birthdays in Miss MacLennan's classroom, and still Michael dared to hope there might be something from Maria. He got up at six o'clock in the morning and went clumping down the stairs to the living room.

'Well, boy, no need to wake you today!'

His grandfather was turning a peat on the fire and he wasn't looking at Michael at all, but the boy knew he was smiling just the same. There on his breakfast plate was a little packet. It wasn't well wrapped (his grandfather couldn't be bothered with silly things like fancy paper and ribbons and tape). It was some strange-shaped object roughly covered with paper, and there was no card beside it.

'Is that my present?' Michael asked, his eyes on the breakfast plate.

'Well, it might be, it might be,' his grandfather murmured, a twinkle in his eye as he turned round. 'Yes, that's from Jess and myself, and it would be from your granny too if she were still with us. But you're not going to open it until you've had your porridge, boy.'

Before that his grandfather fed Jess, brought in some fresh peats for the fire, cleaned his boots, searched for his spectacles and then made the tea. By the time the porridge arrived Michael was hardly able to sit down. He'd looked at the parcel from three hundred and sixty five different angles, and his hands were itching to lift it and guess what it might be. Finally his grandfather sat down in his own

old chair and poured some milk into his cup. That was the
way he ate his porridge, he didn't pour the milk onto it but
took a spoonful from the cup and then dipped it into the
porridge. That way the milk stayed ice cold and the porridge
piping hot.

Well, that morning Michael ate his porridge in ten and
a half seconds.

'Can I open my present now?' he asked.

His grandfather smiled and nodded. Jess lifted her head from beside the fireplace and seemed to be saying yes too.

Michael had the paper off his parcel in less time than it takes to crack an egg, and he gave a gasp when he saw what his present was. A little telescope, no longer than the distance between his elbow and the end of his middle finger, with shining brass edges and a little case the colour of ripe horse chestnuts. Michael put it to his eye and focused on his grandfather, who winked and took another spoonful of porridge.

'That belonged to my grandfather, boy. It's a hundred and sixteen years old, so it's seen a few things in its time. I thought you would look after it better than me.'

Michael was still lost for words. It was the most wonderful gift he could have imagined. He kept turning the little telescope round and round in his hands, unable to believe it was his. Normally his grandfather liked him to say please and thank you for everything, but this morning he didn't seem to mind. He smiled and understood. He didn't take it to school all the same. Someone would drop it or damage it – it was too precious to be passed round by all the boys, even though there was part of him that wished he could do it. They'd be so envious.

Instead he waited until the school day was over and he'd thrown his bag in the corner of his bedroom. He took his telescope, called to Jess, and went chasing up the road to the north end as fast as his legs would carry him. He sat there, getting his breath back, looking out at Reneval and Skarva. It was the first day there had been a little bit of blue sky in weeks, and with the telescope he could see the gannets plummeting into the sea for fish. They were so white, like giant snowflakes.

He felt happier than he had done for a long, long time. It was going to be fried haddock for supper, his very favourite meal. Here he was at his very favourite place in the world on his birthday, holding his precious present in his hands. He looked through the telescope and saw the entrance to his secret cave, there at the bottom of the highest point on the island. The only thing that was wrong was Maria. He had to find a way to make her understand. He had to find treasure for her – to say he was sorry and make peace with her again. It was the one thing he had to do.

5

WELL, Christmas came and went. He missed his father particularly although he wasn't sure why. He hadn't forgotten Maria, but he had all but given up hope of winning her back. Only when he looked at the gold coin and held it in his palm did he remember and think about the treasure and that he could find her.

His grandfather had been told by his doctor that he had to give up smoking his pipe. The old man went down to the jetty for a last time with his pipe at the corner of his mouth. He stood there with old Macaskill for a long time, letting odd puffs of brown smoke lift into the air and disappear. The two of them didn't say a word to each other. Then when he was finished, he took the pipe from his mouth and flung it with all his might into the sea. Then he turned and came back home.

Michael and Jess noticed the difference all right. He was grumpy about the porridge, grumpy about the fire, grumpy about the television, grumpy about the weather. He spent a lot of time just sitting in his chair staring. His bad cough disappeared, but so did his sense of humour.

One Saturday afternoon in January that was exactly where he was. Michael tried hard to think of something that might cheer him up, but in the end he gave up. He couldn't stand sitting here any longer – he had to get out.

'I'm going up to the library – I'll be back in an hour or so.'

Normally his grandfather would remind him he had to get the eggs from the farm, that there was homework to be done and the table to set in the evening. Now he just stared into the fire and grunted.

The library was up at the top of the hill road and Michael hadn't been there more than three times in his life. He made sure that George, Fergus and Ewan weren't any- where in sight when he leaned his bicycle against the outside wall. But who should he see inside the moment he opened the door but Jenny Mackay. Her whole face lit up with smiling.

'Hello, Michael Macgregor. What are you doing here?'

Michael found himself close up against a shelf of books backing away from Jenny Mackay with her big round glasses and freckled face. Her glasses made her eyes look much bigger than they really were.

'Ah, I'm looking for a book,' he said, wishing he'd never come.

'Well,' she said eagerly, coming even closer, 'we've got history here, and geography over there, and if it's stories you're wanting then there are lots of great books across under the window. Would you like me to help you find something, Michael?'

'Jenny, can you come and stack these, please?'

To Michael's relief, the librarian had appeared behind her desk. Jenny must be helping her for the day. She smiled, obviously sorry she had to leave, and turned to go and help. Michael breathed a long sigh of relief. If Fergus had seen him with Jenny Mackay. . . He didn't know what he was looking for, but he pretended he did. He was in the history section and all the books smelled brown and musty. He couldn't read some of the covers at all. He didn't much like history at school. He could understand learning about people and the things they had done, but the history of faraway countries didn't feel important. It was all gone anyway, so what was the point of learning it?

The librarian coughed. He looked round and saw her watching him for a second – there was no-one else in the building at all. Jenny was still stacking shelves, chatting away to herself. He had to find something to read or else escape as fast as possible. His heart hammered as his eye ranged over the old books. He pulled one out and read the dusty title, *An Account of the Parish of Port Ganasdale and the History of the Surrounding District*. Michael could understand why people didn't come into libraries! The librarian coughed again and his eyes started searching once more as he crammed the book back on its shelf. There had to be something. . .

He pulled out a thicker book with a stronger cover at the very bottom of the shelf. He crouched there and opened it. *A History of the Island of Coolin*. He couldn't believe his good fortune – he'd never heard of such a book before! He got up and went over to one of the desks and pulled out a chair. Three bicycles went whizzing past on the track outside and he knew at once who they belonged to. But he didn't want to be outside, there was plenty of time to be out later. He opened the book, careful of its thin and fragile pages.

The first chapter was very boring, all about the first people to live on Coolin, the things they'd made and how they survived. There was a long section on the first church and where it had been. The next went on and on about fishing. He was almost in despair when suddenly he found a chapter almost at the very end, all stories connected with the island. That was better. The librarian and Jenny were talking together at the back of the library; now he had time to read in peace. There were stories about seals and about an old man who'd lived in a cave at the south end of the island. There were stories about a well and people who had been healed by its water. Then there were stories about the north end. . .

> 'There are still people alive on Coolin with tales of a ship from the Spanish Armada that vanished in a storm at the north end of the island. They say that the ship disappeared under the hill, but how this is possible they cannot explain. Many searches have been made of the surrounding beaches and not a single piece of evidence has been found to support the story.'

Michael could have shrieked for joy. Suddenly his hope was restored. The story of the Spanish galleon and the north end was more alive than it had been, the story he had first heard from old Morag. Suddenly too his dream of finding the ship returned, and of doing it not alone but with Maria. He felt dizzy with joy and he read the passage in the book over and over again to make sure his eyes had not deceived him.

'Do you need any help finding a book?'

He nearly jumped out of his skin. The librarian was standing on tiptoe at her desk, looking at him suspiciously. Hastily he pushed the history book on to the shelf and looked at her.

'Ah, no, I was just looking for something. But do you by any chance have anything on boats for my grandfather?'

The librarian looked at him even more frostily. 'We have three hundred and fifty two books on boats. What sort of book on boats is it you're wanting?'

Michael racked his brains, panicking. He had spoken the first words that came into his head, he hadn't been thinking.

'Ah, something funny,' he said, swallowing hard.

'Something funny,' the librarian said, in a voice that sounded anything but funny. She bent down to look at a shelf and all Michael could see of her was her bottom. Jenny stopped stacking shelves and looked over at him and grinned. The librarian reappeared, a bit like a duck coming up for air in a duck pond.

'Here's something you could take him. It's a book called *Three Men in a Boat*. I'll have to give you a library card – I've never seen you here before.'

Michael sneaked out without any of the boys seeing him. He breathed a sigh of relief as he whizzed home on his bicycle, the book tucked safely under his right arm. He was still thinking about what he'd read – he felt happier than he'd done for longer than he could remember.

His grandfather was still sitting miserably in his chair when Michael came in. He wasn't sure who looked more unhappy – his grandfather or Jess. Michael sat down opposite him.

'I brought you a book from the library,' he said.

His grandfather grunted, didn't even raise his head. Michael put the book in his lap. He didn't so much as look at the title. Suddenly the boy dared ask a question that had been in his mind for ages.

'What's the best gift you can get for a girl?' he asked.

His grandfather looked at him mournfully. 'Flowers.'

6

IT WAS the fourteenth of February and he hadn't got a Valentine's Card. He really hadn't expected one anyway, so it was no great surprise. He'd been woken at seven o'clock that Saturday morning by the sound of his grandfather laughing. It wasn't just a chuckle, it was a real hoot of laughter. He woke up with the loudness of it and couldn't get back to sleep. Michael was extremely puzzled. His grandfather had been in the doldrums for days now and the last thing he expected to hear from him was laughter. When he was pulling on his jumper at a quarter past eight there was another great gale of laughter. He was mystified.

He thudded downstairs, frowning as he scratched himself sleepily. He was a bit annoyed at being woken so early. There was his grandfather reading beside the fire.

'This is a cracking book you brought me!' he exclaimed, jabbing the page with his finger. 'I haven't read anything so funny in forty years. Would you make the breakfast, boy?'

So Michael heated the porridge and made the toast while his grandfather hooted and slapped his thigh and ruffled Jess's coat. His face was a bright red colour Michael had seen only once before after he and George from Campbeltown finished off a bottle of whisky together at New Year. Even Jess looked puzzled.

'That was Puffin Billy with the mail,' his grandfather told him when Michael came through with the porridge. He didn't even look up from the book. 'Would you get the mail, boy?' Michael went out to the porch and picked three letters up from the mat. Maybe there would be a red heart on the back of one of them. . . He brought them in bitterly and slapped them on the table. His grandfather looked round at him.

'You look as if you'd eaten a pound of green cheese, boy. If it's Valentine's Day that's worrying you, I wouldn't. There's always next year and there are plenty of fish in the sea. Have you seen a haddock you particularly like, boy?'

Michael fussed with the porridge bowls and felt his cheeks going red. Fortunately his grandfather had to finish a paragraph.

'Well, here's one girl that won't fail you, boy.' Jess lifted her head and her ears stuck up like sails. 'You take her a good walk and she'll not forget it. It's going to be a nice day.'

His grandfather was right. There were long trails of blue sky in the window, and a band of sunlight stretched over the sea. It was the first good day in months. Michael ate as though his life depended on it, rushed upstairs to find his telescope and came back in with Jess's lead dangling from one hand. Jess rushed out from the fireside like a black and white waterfall and nearly knocked the precious book onto the floor. Out in the street Michael heard another long gale of laughter. It was amazing. He couldn't remember the last time his grandfather had picked up a book, let alone had his nose in one. There was a difference about everything. He realised he didn't need a jumper at all, he'd be far too warm. It was the first day of Spring. The sea was like glass, there wasn't a ripple on it. The faraway islands were clear and sharp; it was as if he could have stretched his fingers to touch them. He heard a wave wash against the village shore. It was the only sound in the world that morning. All at once Michael wanted to be out of the village while it was still that quiet. He got to the north end in record time and had to collapse in a sand dune to get his breath back. Jess jumped down beside him and scattered a whole shower of sand over him with her paws.

'You stupid beast,' he wailed, rubbing the sand out of his eyes. 'You're some present for Valentine's Day!'

Jess looked at him sheepishly, not understanding what she'd done wrong. Michael lay down in the sand and closed his eyes; now it didn't matter in the least getting more sand in his hair. When he opened his eyes again he could see the high hill over at the far end of the bay. It was shaped like a great pudding, and it was all heathery and rocky on top. It was strange to think it was the highest point on Coolin.

He thought to himself about Morag's story and the coin she had given him; he thought too about the words he'd read in the old history book in the library. The book had said that the ship had disappeared under the hill. He got up onto his elbows and ruffled Jess's ears with one hand, still looking at the hill and thinking. It just didn't make sense, none of it made any sense at all.

Suddenly he decided he'd go over and have a look. No-one really bothered to climb to the top usually, apart from tourists. There was a little pile of stones at the summit called a cairn, and on a good day you could see all sorts of islands from the top. But now Michael decided he was going to go to the top – he had plenty of time and it was a beautiful morning. The skies were getting clearer all the time.

He ran over the beach with Jess at his heels and started climbing the steep bank on the far side. It was hard work and he was out of breath before he was even a quarter of the way up. The wind was strong; it seemed to gust from nowhere and blow away all your energy. Jess looked as if she was being dried by a giant hairdryer when the wind gusted like that and Michael laughed at her. She looked at him with puzzled eyes as the black and white hair was blown over her face.

'You look very silly,' he said, and bent down to make a fuss of her. The two of them struggled on up the hill. The heather was deep, and every time you took a step you went up to your waist in it. The heather was like a kind of sea. It took him much longer than he had imagined to get up close to the top. In fact if he had known just how long it might take him he probably wouldn't have gone to begin with. At last he was almost there and the heather wasn't deep at all now, it was no higher than his ankles. He decided he would go as far as the cairn of stones on the very summit and see what he could see.

Just then he caught a glimpse of something at his feet. A flash of something, a flicker. He took a couple of steps backwards and Jess waited for him, blown out by the wind. There were some stones in the ground, and there was a gap between them. He moved back and forth to try to see if he could catch sight of whatever it was that had shone, but there was nothing. He even put his head down close to the stones, but now he could see only blackness.

He went over to the cairn and realised it was almost right at the edge of a steep drop. Below him, the sea came crashing onto the rocks in white foam. He wanted so much to believe that one of the ships from the Armada had come to Coolin, that there was real treasure on his island. Miss

MacLennan had told them about the Spanish Armada. She had said that stories of ships with treasure were nonsense, that all of them had been built for fighting and that they would never have carried gold and jewels.

Michael had been tempted to bring his coin in then, just to prove her wrong. But something always stopped him, and somehow he didn't think she wanted to believe anyway. He went back down the way he'd come and stopped again about the point where he'd seen the flash of light. He was certain he hadn't imagined it; he was completely sure. Somehow it had been far below him, not right under his foot. But that didn't make sense, none of it made sense. He got out his little telescope and looked at Reneval and Skarva. He could see the seals sunning themselves on Skarva; they looked like giant slugs with their tails turned up into the air. He could see every single rock with the telescope.

Suddenly he thought of Maria and he felt a pain in his heart at the memory of her. He sat down on the ground there at the top of Coolin and he went over it all in his mind for the seven hundredth time. He looked down onto the north end beach and remembered that morning when they sat together in the cave. He'd called to her to come back as she ran away crying over the beach. Her footsteps had been washed out by the tide long ago, but he hadn't forgotten her for a moment. He just didn't know what to do. He couldn't think what would win her back or how he would do it. He wasn't sure what mattered more to him – to find the Spanish galleon or to win back Maria. There was no difference between them in his mind.

That evening George, Fergus and Ewan arrived at the door. He had a dish towel in his hand. George shook his head.

'Look at that. Who'd have believed it. Do you think he knits as well?'

Michael flicked the dish towel at him and just missed his nose. 'There are still some to be done, George. You can come in and do them if you want.'

Fergus kicked a stone over the road and it cartwheeled down onto the shore.

'No, we wondered if maybe you fancied a barbeque at the beach. But if you're too busy doing housework. . .'

Michael opened the door a little further and looked inside towards the armchair.

'On you go, boy. Come back before it's dark, though, and don't go and give that dog too many sausages. I'll be fine. I've got the last chapter of my book to read.'

Jess had come out from the fireside when she heard the word 'sausages'. They all laughed and made a fuss of her ears. Together the five of them set off for the beach. It was a beautiful night. The sky to the north and west was a clear blue, almost white. There was one star there like a single drop of gold. They dragged up great big bits of wood from the shore and soon had a great orange fire burning. The sausages were pretty black but no-one minded, certainly not Jess.

Michael felt happy for the first time in a long while. The year was beginning again at last and the long summer

lay ahead of them. If he could find a way to win back Maria
that would be everything. But it looked like being no easier
than finding the Spanish galleon.

7

THAT HAD BEEN the first day of Spring. After that the weeks seemed to rush by on Coolin as the island came alive after the winter. Old Macaskill landed three big lobsters and gave one of them to Michael's grandfather. The old man ruffled his grandson's hair and grinned.

'We're going to enjoy it, boy! We're going to enjoy it and Jess can chew the claws if she likes! This is one lobster that's not going to end up on a table on the Costa del Sol! And you know why, boy? Because this is a thank you to you. Yes, it was you that got me to forget that old pipe of mine with the book you brought home from the library!'

They ate the lobster between them and it tasted good, but like nothing Michael had ever had before. He dreamed that night of exploring rock pools under the sea. He could hear the waves rushing in his ears and when he woke up in the morning and lay there in the half dark he wasn't sure if he was a boy who had dreamed he was a seal or a seal who had dreamed he was a boy.

Everywhere on Coolin there were lambs. The air was loud with their bleating and although they looked lovely, like beautifully knitted toys, they were as stupid as their parents. A lamb got stuck on Murdo's roof (nobody knew how it got there) and it bleated all night until Murdo himself – who was ninety four – went out in his pyjamas and got it down. He was very tempted to keep that lamb for chops but in the end he didn't. In April a new doctor came to live on Coolin. Everyone was talking about her because she was young and blonde, and very cheery and not like a doctor at all. One day Michael's grandfather announced he had something wrong with his left foot.

'Since when?'

'Och, well, I think I twisted it coming home from Macaskill's the other evening.' Michael's grandfather rubbed his foot.

'I thought you said it was your left foot?'

'I did, boy, I did.'

'Then why is it you're holding the right one?'

Anyway, his grandfather hobbled up the road to see the new doctor the following Tuesday afternoon, though whether he remembered what was wrong with him at all by the time he reached the surgery Michael wasn't sure. He certainly came back looking much better, his cheeks glowing pink. Michael remembered that it had been all but impossible getting him to go to see Dr Fitzpatrick in past years; even when his foot was green with poison he didn't want to go. It was only when Old Macaskill had muttered the word gangrene that he very reluctantly went along to see what the Quack had to say.

It would soon be the holidays and Michael was counting the days. He'd been working harder, trying to keep on the right side of Miss MacLennan, and she seemed to notice that. At least she hadn't shouted at him as she did the year before, or made fun of him in front of the whole class.

One morning he saw something strange. He was coming in early and his heart lifted because there was Maria leaving her bike at the back of the school. Then he saw her wiping her cheeks, brushing something away. Two older girls walked off, looking smug and smirking, and he wondered what had happened. He didn't want to stare but he was almost sure she had been crying. What had they said to her? He wanted to ask her if she was all right but he couldn't summon the courage. She would brush him away as she had done before and he would just look a fool. His mouth was dry and he couldn't think. He hurried away inside before she came back, his heart thudding.

He wished all morning he had done something; he wished he'd had the courage. He watched her as she sat in front of him and he wondered what she was thinking and feeling. He knew that she was a loner, that she didn't really have friends. Was that what they had been making fun of her about? She had looked so very unhappy. And that made him remember the awful day up at the north end all those months ago when he asked her about her mother without thinking and she ran away. It was the last time he had spoken to her. He looked at her bowed head and long gold hair and was determined he would find her something, and so discover a way to win her back too.

That Saturday he decided to go fishing to the loch. His grandfather was reading a book and Jess was at his feet. It wasn't a good day; the rain was splintering against the windows and there was a real wind, though it wasn't cold now. Michael felt restless and came down about eleven, his rod and some lunch all packed.

'So we're having trout tonight, Jess?' he said, rubbing the collie's ears. 'Well, I hope you catch more than a cold, boy, I wouldn't want to be out on the moor this afternoon. And certainly not with my bad foot.'

'I thought the new doctor made it better?' Michael said.

Michael's grandfather disappeared muttering into his book.

'If I'm not back by six, just send Jess out to look for me.'

'Take my crook with you, boy. It's rough walking. No, don't look at me like that. You don't want to have a broken leg for all the six weeks of the school holidays.'

He was glad to be outside; it didn't matter about the rain. He stood for a minute listening to the quiet. A small boat hummed like a bee round one of the points – it was Old Macaskill searching for more lobsters. The wind came up and the waves were rippled. There was mist up on the top of Coolin, up where he was going, and the hill at the north end would be totally swallowed by now.

It was a perfect day for fishing. For a minute Michael thought of his cousin Angus living in Glasgow, in the very middle of all that noise and rush. Whenever Angus came to visit they argued like cat and dog over which place was better. They got on quite well about everything else, but not what the best place in the world was. Well, you could keep Glasgow, Michael thought to himself that morning. Angus could have his Glasgow.

He went up between the village houses, his grandfather's old crook tapping on the road as he went. He'd almost thought of leaving the silly thing behind, but his grandfather would be sure to ask him about it later and he didn't want to offend him. On the way past the shop he saw Morag coming towards him. He'd hardly seen her since that evening the previous year when he went to visit and she'd given him the precious coin.

'Well, and how are you Donald?' she asked, stopping in front of him, her blind eyes searching his face. Donald was his grandfather's name and for a moment Michael was puzzled.

'No, it's me, Morag, it's Michael,' he said, reddening.

Her face burst into smiling and then she rocked with laughter.

'It's because you had that old stick of your grandfather's!' she exclaimed. 'And where are you off to?'

He smiled, and she could hear him smiling. 'Fishing.'

She put a hand on his arm. 'Well, leave a nice fish on my back doorstep for MacTavish and me,' she said more quietly and was on her way again. All these fish he had to catch – he'd better be in luck today. And he hadn't fished for ages.

Up on the moor it felt like a different world. The mist closed in like cotton wool and you couldn't see the sea, not in any direction. It felt eerie and lonely, but it was a good loneliness all the same. The breeze was strong in his face and he had to trudge round to the far side to have the wind behind him. He was just deciding on the best bit of the bank to have a first go when suddenly he noticed something.

The sun had come out for a moment from behind the mist. In a second it turned the little loch gold, and Michael had to shade his eyes because the water was sore to look at. But it made him notice something once the sun was hidden again. Out on the loch there were lilies, white water lilies. They grew there every year and no-one really took the slightest notice of them. They were just another part of the landscape of Coolin. But the more Michael stood there the more he thought, and he remembered the words of his grandfather. He had an idea.

He dropped his rod but kept the crook, his grandfather's old stick, tight in his left hand. It was a good bit longer than he was, and that was just what he wanted. He half ran to the nearest point of land at the end of the loch. The mist had come back – now the lilies were the only thing of colour in all the grey. They had beautiful golden hearts surrounded by white leaves. They looked a bit like hands folded together. But the problem was they were too far out.

His grandfather had told him stories about children from Coolin who had drowned trying to get water lilies. They always grew tantalisingly close to the shore, just out of reach. It wasn't the flowers that were dangerous, it was their long stalks under the water. The risk came when you swam out to pick them; your feet caught in them and you got tangled and dragged down and down in the mud. Michael shivered. He leaned out with the crook from the end of the point. The nearest lily was still out of reach, but not by much. He looked all round for an idea. Then he saw a large boulder a little way away, and he dropped the crook. The stone weighed a ton and he had to roll it, end over end, up to the edge of the water. Then he managed to push it another step forward.

Now he picked up the crook again, his hands shaking. He hoped against hope it would be enough. He leaned out over the water and the crook reached round the stalk of the lily. He pulled. Nothing happened. He reached out a little further and a little deeper and pulled again, more strongly this time. There was a rush of water and there was the lily, held in the handle of the crook. It had worked after all!

In the end he got three water lilies. The third one all but pulled him into the loch and he got one foot very wet. He decided he had been lucky and that it was best to quit while he was ahead. He hadn't even had one try for a fish before he turned for home, the three lilies clutched safely in one hand.

In the village shop he bought two tins of tuna. He leaned his fishing rod against the outside door at home and decided not to disturb his grandfather. He would see him later. He kept the lilies with him and cycled over to Morag's farm at Claddich. He had promised her a fish, so he left the tin of tuna on her doorstep as a present. He could hear her laughing already. It was raining hard by the time he got back and his grandfather wasn't in the house. Michael decided that now was the time. He went upstairs with the lilies and found a paper and pen. What was he to write?

All sorts of things went through his head but nothing seemed right. He had no confidence to say anything, he was too frightened of making a fool of himself. In the end he simply wrote, 'from Michael'.

Suddenly he heard the door opening downstairs. He hurried downstairs and brushed past Jess and his grandfather, not even stopping for his coat. His grandfather called after him, mystified, but Michael was gone. The rain was coming down in grey sheets, but it was a warm rain and he didn't mind. It was singing from the roofs and the gutters and it glistened on his hands. He ran all the way to the manse and left the lilies on the front step, where Maria would be sure to find them. He waited a second before turning and running home as fast as his legs would carry him. He felt something in his pocket. It was the other tin of tuna, for their supper that night.

8

THAT MONDAY he waited, looking forward to Maria's face. Perhaps she would say sorry for having been silent for so many months, maybe she would even slip him a note in class. He felt a warm glow in his tummy that stayed with him all the way to school. It was a beautiful day and he felt happy.

But it wasn't like that. Maria dumped her bag beside her seat and didn't look near him when she came in. Her hair was tied in a tight knot and her back was straight and she never turned round. There was no note, nor was there a look or the faintest hint of a smile. He almost felt that she was angry.

Michael went home at lunch-time understanding nothing. He felt numb and sick. The warm glow had gone – he felt foolish and confused. He heard footsteps chasing at his back and glanced round. It was Fergus and he slapped Michael on the back. He could hardly breathe for running and his face was red like a boiled lobster.

'Are you coming to football, coming to football this afternoon?' he gasped, getting the words out in bits and pieces.

Michael wanted to say yes but he shook his head. 'No,

I'll not manage,' he said bleakly. He was almost at his grand-father's door.

Fergus looked puzzled and exhausted. He was still panting for breath. 'I ran all that way for nothing!' he said frustrated, and turned away.

At lunch Michael felt even bleaker for having said no to football. He bit his lettuce angrily and stared moodily at the table cloth.

'What's wrong with you, boy? Is it women?'

Michael sighed heavily. 'I don't want to talk about it, grandpa.' He could feel his eyes stinging with sharp tears. He had hoped so much that this would make a difference, that a gift like that would change her mind and win her back. But what if she had never got the lilies at all? What if something had happened to them or her father had thrown them out?

'You know I remember once your grandmother was angry with me, boy.' The old man had put down his knife and fork, and pushed back his chair. He was looking out to somewhere over the sea, and the light shone on his blue eyes. Michael tried hard not to listen but he couldn't help doing so all the same. His grandfather had a habit of talking to him even when he knew Michael didn't want him to.

'I had come in with muddy feet,' he went on. 'It was a wild October night and I had been out helping Macaskill with his boat. If there was one thing your grandmother hated it was dirty feet in the house. In the old days before you came here I had to take my shoes off as soon as I came into the house – rain, hail or shine. Well, those boots of mine were muddy. Yes, I know you have to go back to school after lunch, boy, but this won't take more than two minutes to tell. In I came at nine o'clock and I had muddy feet in every room in the house. And you know what she did? She threw a bowl of potato peelings over me, she was that mad!'

Michael couldn't help but smile. He tried to hide it by eating a biscuit.

'Well, I was angry too. I slept down here by the fire that night beside Jess, nursing my wrath to keep it warm! But you know, the next morning I woke up at dawn. I was wide awake and could remember every bit of what had happened the evening before. I went out and down on to the beach. I found some shells for your granny and I brought them back and laid them on her pillow. And I said I was sorry for my muddy boots.'

Michael wasn't sure what to say. His grandfather was still looking out to sea, and there was a kind of glistening in his eyes and he was nodding all the time. Michael wanted to say something but he couldn't find the words. He didn't feel too bad now, that was true. A long way away he heard a bell ringing. He scraped back his chair in a hurry.

'That's the school bell, grandpa! I have to go. I'll get you those library books on the way home.'

That night in the dark he thought about Maria again, and about the precious lilies he'd got for her. He thought too about the story his grandfather had told him. The thing was that Maria hadn't accepted the gift he had got for her, that was the difference. His grandmother had. He wished his mother was there to ask, he wished he could have talked

67

to her about it all. There was simply nothing more he could do, that was the truth of it. He had tried and he had failed. For some reason there was nothing he could do to make it right again. Michael didn't even feel angry any more, just empty. He went to sleep and he dreamed of nothing at all.

That Wednesday was the last day before the holidays. Michael's grandfather was reading a book in the kitchen when the boy came down to breakfast. He was stirring the porridge with his left hand and holding the book in his right.

'Ah, you have to read Robert Louis Stevenson, boy, you would love it! Pirates and treasure galleons – all the things you dream of!'

Michael slumped down in his chair. Somehow Morag's gold coin and all the old stories meant nothing now. They had been stories he shared with Maria and now she was gone. Without her they felt empty and useless. But he couldn't tell his grandfather all that; he couldn't tell anyone at all. They wouldn't understand.

When he went into the classroom plans were being hatched in every corner. Someone was going on a fishing trip to Reneval and Skarva; two others in the class were off to stay with cousins in Glasgow. Even Miss MacLennan was in a good mood and did a quiz with them instead of the usual Wednesday maths. At lunch-time, when the last school bell went, Michael gathered up his things bitterly and went out into the corridor. Most of the rest had burst through the main doors already, running for all they were worth, even though Mr Stewart was shouting for them to walk until they had got to the gates. It was too late.

Michael walked mournfully out past the bike sheds. There was a whole group of girls there, gathered in a tight knot. He saw someone being pushed, and several of them laughing. He slowed down, forgetting his own sadness, wondering what was going on.

'You'll certainly not do anything exciting in the holidays, will you? Not with a boring old minister for a father!'

'Yeah, where are you going for the summer, Maria? Church?'

There was another gale of laughter and Michael saw Maria's face. He remembered what he had seen before. His heart was hammering.

'Leave her alone.'

The white faces of the older girls turned to look at him surprised. They hadn't seen him before. He was shaking.

'Nothing to do with you, MacGregor. Haven't you got a home to go to?'

His mouth was dry and dusty. He felt dizzy there in the sunlight. Now he saw Maria's face again. She was looking right at him, her eyes huge and afraid. She was hemmed in by the other girls.

'Leave her alone,' he said again, his voice croaky.

'Yeah, and what are you going to do about it, MacGregor?' one girl said, coming forward towards him, her face sour. She was a girl who was always in trouble. Her name was Sonya.

'I'll tell her father,' Michael suddenly said, and they all heard him. He had no idea where the words came from;

they were just suddenly there without him planning them. Sonya stopped in her tracks and just looked at him, as if she wasn't sure what to do. One of the other girls was shuffling a stone with her foot, looking down at the ground. Someone else sighed heavily.

'Come on, girls, we'd better leave them to it. I reckon he fancies her, that's why he's sticking up for her.'

Sonya gave him a last look and began walking away. The knot of girls reluctantly began breaking up and following her. Michael suddenly woke out of his trance and started off in the other direction, away from the school and away from the village, round towards the shore. He had no real idea where he was going, he just knew he had to get away. That was all that mattered. He went and sat on the rocks; watched some black fins of fish chasing in a rock pool below him. It looked as though it was going to be a fine afternoon. He thought about what he'd seen and heard. He felt sick.

They had bullied him for a bit in the class, when he first came. That was because he was new and had come from the mainland, and because he'd joined the class in the middle of the year. But once he made friends with George, Fergus and Ewan it had all stopped. It was as if he was accepted then, was all right. Why hadn't Maria fought back, tried to defend herself? He hoped she was all right now, but he didn't dare follow her to the manse to find out. She would just cold shoulder him anyway. She didn't want to have anything to do with him.

It was the holidays. Suddenly the thought sank in for

the first time and he smiled to himself. There would be good things to do all the same. He took a stone and skimmed it over the surface of the water. The first jumps were easy to see but after six he lost count; the last four or five all ran into each other.

Suddenly he remembered something; the memory jumped out at him from nowhere. Skimming stones was one of the last things he'd done with his father, before the accident. His hand felt as if it had been stung and he didn't look for any more stones. He stood up tall and looked out over the sea. It was so still, so amazingly still. He felt too warm. The faraway sky was the strangest colour, a kind of oily yellow. It was as though he could see all the way to America. And there wasn't a breath of wind. He was too warm and the air was woolly to breathe. He heard a boat humming over the sea somewhere very, very far away. The air was so still that boat could have been hundreds of miles away.

Maria was lost to him now. There was no use worrying about her or wishing he could change things. He had tried and he had failed. The lilies were the best gift he could have thought of, and she might as well have brought them back to his front door and flung them in his face. He had to get over it. He had made a fool of himself. But at least no-one else knew, at least it was his secret. He was glad he hadn't told his grandfather. That had been for the best.

He walked back the way he had come. It was funny walking past the classroom; Miss MacLennan had even left up one of the questions from the quiz – What was the name of the mythical land of gold? El Dorado. He thought about the gold coin Morag had given him, and the story of the treasure ship. He remembered too what Maria had told him about her family, that they were supposed to be related to the shipwrecked sailors. He leaned his head against the windowsill. He could see his seat, and Maria's in front. Now they were all gone, and it was as if everything else had gone too – all the dreams he longed for. He did not believe in treasure either – he did not believe in anything at all that afternoon.

He trailed slowly home, too warm and too listless to hurry. He looked out to sea and he didn't believe he'd ever seen the other islands so clearly before. They seemed close enough to touch, and the water was like pale glass with a yellow sheen.

'So your grandfather has to put up with you for six weeks?' said Old Macaskill coming out of the shop. He ruffled his hair cheerfully. Old Macaskill had about three teeth left, so when he drank whisky not even he understood what he was saying.

'It's me who has to put up with him for six weeks,' said Michael. He gave the sheepdog Dawn a clap before going the last bit home.

Soon Coolin would be busy with tourists again, all wanting ice cream and postcards. He remembered suddenly that a couple of years ago a tourist from America had bumped into Fergus and asked him where he could get a film for his camera. Fergus thought about this long and hard and looked out to sea. At last he knew the answer. He pointed to the tiny island of Skarva, which was hardly big enough for two sheep, and said he thought that would be the best place to get a film. The tourist went away quite happy, thanking him for his help.

Michael let Dawn go on seeking out exciting smells at the top of the jetty. He wanted to get rid of his schoolbag and his jumper – he was far too hot.

He went inside and almost bumped into his grandfather in the porch.

'You change and come and help me, boy,' he said. His face was white and his eyes big with worry. 'There's a mighty storm coming.'

9

MICHAEL staggered into the living room. He couldn't believe his ears.

'What d'you mean? I've just been over at the beach – it's a beautiful day.'

His grandfather took two strides and switched on the radio on the table. He looked at Michael with eyes like marbles.

'. . . The Western Isles is expected to bear the brunt of hurricane force winds coming in from the Atlantic this evening. People are being urged only to make the most urgent of journeys and there are particular concerns for communities on the western edges of the islands. John McGill of Glasgow University is one of those concerned by the suddenness and severity of the storm, coming as it does in the middle of summer, and his fear is that this is yet another sign of global warming. Professor McGill joins us in the studio this afternoon. Professor McGill. . .'

Michael's grandfather clicked off the radio triumphantly, his eyes still fixed on the boy.

'Now do you need to hear any more than that? And I

didn't learn it from the radio either. Morag's cattle were behaving strangely early this morning, as if they were sensing something we couldn't. Now, come on, we're going to help Macaskill with the boat!'

Michael went chasing upstairs. He didn't need to be told twice. He was shaking as never before in his life, and seemed to be all fingers and thumbs. Cupboards were difficult to open and nothing was where he wanted it to be. He muttered to himself under his breath and his heart knocked at his chest so hard he thought it would fall out.

'Come on, boy. We have to hurry!' For once he didn't answer his grandfather back. He wouldn't have known what to say anyway. At last he was ready, his hair sticking in the air like a hedgehog's prickles, but that didn't matter. He found himself outside, calling to Jess to get in, his voice hoarse and severe. Suddenly he found Jenny Mackay beside him, her hair flying about her in the breeze. She was smiling, to his great surprise she was smiling, trying to say something about his hair.

'You have to get home, Jenny,' he cried, not listening to what she was saying. 'You have to get home. There's a terrible storm coming!'

Her face changed and she was saying something, but he couldn't make it out. She had turned and was tearing away back up the street, calling something. Suddenly his grandfather was there beside him. He couldn't remember when he had last seen his grandfather running, but the old man ran that afternoon just the same. He had on his bright orange jacket and he ran all the way to Macaskill's house at the far side of the village. He burst into the house.

The three of them dragged up the boat between them. Well, Michael and his grandfather did most of the work, and Macaskill shouted orders. Michael glanced once out to the end of the Roo, the Point, and he saw the colour of the sea and the waves that were curling in to the island. And this was nothing to what it would be . . .

When they were done with the boat, his grandfather grabbed his arm.

'We need to see how Morag is!' he shouted.

Michael nodded, remembering too. His mind was racing.

'I'll cycle over, help her with anything she needs doing!'

'Good lad!'

He began running up over the top of the beach. It felt special hearing these words from his grandfather. He was so used to being called 'boy' by him, and though he knew he meant the word kindly, to be called 'lad' was different. The echo of the words stayed with him until he found his bicycle and leapt on to it.

Someone was gathering their hens. Two people were running across a field carrying something. Michael was cycling against the wind, over to Claddich that was on the west side of the island, and the gusts were getting stronger all the time. When he'd first heard his grandfather mention the storm and he'd heard the voice on the radio it had almost seemed exciting. It wasn't real then. But now it was different, it was really beginning. He cycled for all he was worth over the hill and never had it seemed so far to Claddich. His knees hurt so badly he could hardly keep going. He could hear the waves coming over the beach, even though they were still a long way away. He had never heard them from here. He left his bicycle with the wheels spinning and skidded up the path to Morag's door. He rapped on it and opened it, breathless.

'Mercy me! Who's that?' Morag's face was a white oval of worry. For the first time ever Michael really saw that she was blind. Normally she was so full of fun and laughter, and so clever you would never have known she bothered about being blind. Now she was holding the back of a chair as if she was frightened, and she looked smaller than usual. Only MacTavish seemed the same.

'It's me, Michael,' he said when he got his breath back, and he could see the relief spreading over her face. 'I came to see if you needed anything at all, with the storm coming. Maybe you want to come over to be with us in the village.' That was his own idea – it had suddenly come into his mind that she might feel better there, over on the more sheltered side of the island.

She smiled now, her whole face smiled. 'Oh, that's kind of you, Michael, but I'll stay here to keep an eye on everything. Well, an ear at least. But you're a kind soul for coming over. There's one thing you can do for me, though. You can put some bags of sand at the door of my shed, in case the sea comes right up. I'd hate the water to get in. I've so many precious books!'

He nodded, understanding. That was no trouble. He said goodbye, and then remembered to tell her to call anytime if she needed something. She told him he was a kind lad and his ears burned as he went out into the wind. That was the second time today.

It had changed even since he got out to Claddich, he was sure of it. He really had to fight against the wind now – sometimes it seemed stronger than he was. He suddenly thought of those first pictures of men on the moon, for it felt a bit like that. You had to fight to do everything against the wind, so everything took longer. He felt tired putting those bags against the shed door, even though they weren't all that heavy. The door of the shed was thundering in the wind, as if some very angry person on the other side was trying to get out. He was done in the end and he got up. Then he gasped in fear.

Out beyond the edge of the beach, away far out on the edge of the sea, there was a great wall of darkness. It was as if a giant wave was rolling in from the Atlantic, but Michael could see that it was no wave. It was the storm, and it was black as a bruise. Another gust almost knocked him off his feet and it seemed to waken him up. He realised he had to get home, as fast as he possibly could. At least he was going the other way now. The wind helped him, pushed him back towards the village.

Somehow he felt that black cloud behind him; he could sense it was there as if it was watching him. He remembered the words on the radio about global warming and he felt frightened. This was the first day of the summer holidays, there should never be a storm like this. And it had come out of nothing at all. He remembered something his grandfather had told him about his dad. His dad had

had a big shop in Glasgow for outdoor clothing. 'There's no such thing as bad weather,' he used to say, 'just bad clothing.' He wondered what his father would have thought of this, as he pedalled like mad up the last hill before the long drop down to the village. He thought about his mum and dad and felt a stab of pain in his chest. As he spun down the hill towards the shop and the jetty he looked away over to where Maria and her dad lived. He thought about the water lilies and the note, and he thought about what he'd seen earlier that day. He caught a glimpse of a yellow light and then it was gone.

He'd never known the village so quiet. There wasn't a soul about. The shop sign was creaking eerily in the wind. The sea was the only thing he could hear; the waves were coming right up over the jetty, dark and wild. He came skidding round the corner and almost bumped right into his grandfather.

'I was out looking for you, boy! Come in, come in! Leave the bicycle safe in against the wall, you don't want it damaged. They say the Outer Hebrides have been without power for two hours now!'

Michael came inside and shivered, not because he was cold but because of his fear of the storm cloud. Together they barricaded the front door.

'We've enough food for an army, boy, and there's the peat fire for us to make tea and cook food if we lose our power too. We'll do all right, won't we?'

He put his arm round Michael's shoulder, then ruffled his hair.

'What would my dad have said about this storm?' the boy suddenly asked. His grandfather looked at him strangely, his face grey and long. That was the last question he had expected, it was as if all the air had been knocked out of him. He sat down heavily in the armchair and looked into the fire. Then suddenly he looked at Michael, his eyes clear and shining.

'He would say we had to be brave and make the most of it, and he would tell us to remember and wrap up warm. And you know what, boy, that's exactly what we're going to do!'

It felt rather silly getting dressed to go to bed, but they did all the same. They put on about five layers each, but Michael's grandfather told him it was the best way to be. They should be ready if something happened to the house, or if someone needed help outside. Jess looked at them with her head on one side.

All at once there was a terrific boom and they both ducked. There was a blue flash and the living room was left dark except for the orange glow of the fire. The wind was roaring.

'That's really it beginning now,' the old man said quietly.

'Now, off you go to bed, boy, and I'll see you get there safely with a candle. If you want anything just you call me. And if you're frightened, don't try to be braver than you are, all right? This is going to be a big night for us all. And when you get to your bed, say a prayer for the people on the sea. We're the lucky ones on land, that's something I know for sure.'

Michael went upstairs with his red candle. He could feel the whole cottage shaking. There was a sort of rumbling under his feet and he wondered if the walls would be all right. Then he remembered how old it was, that it had been built all the way back in 1762. There had been a lot of storms since then, and it was still standing. He went over the bedroom floor to look out on the sea. It sounded as though hundreds of snakes were writhing on the sea, all trying to get out of the water and on to Coolin. The window was rattling and shaking, banging in the wind as if it was frightened too. His grandfather was right, though. It was worse by far for the people on the sea.

'Please, God, keep them safe,' he whispered as he looked out on to the dark sea. All the lights had gone out and he thought how very different the world was without electricity. It became like the old days, like hundreds of years ago, and suddenly the world felt much bigger too. It seemed like a long, long way to the mainland. 'Please be near to Morag tonight,' he prayed, thinking of her frightened and alone at the farm at Claddich. 'Please keep her animals safe and her books.'

10

SO BEGAN one of the strangest nights of his life. There he was, with all those layers on, under the covers of the bed. He lay on his back and listened. The storm seemed bigger in the darkness. He didn't even dare go to the window and look out now, he just stayed where he was, thinking about many things that were like a storm in his head. He fell into a kind of half sleep.

He dreamed that he was up on the middle of Coolin, close to where he'd gone to get the water lilies. He was running for all he was worth and there was someone ahead of him. The person turned round and he saw it was Maria. He was shouting to her to stop but she couldn't hear him or else she wouldn't listen. She looked so sad when she turned to look at him, but she wouldn't stop running. Then somehow he had run down to Morag's farm and the water had washed right up to the shed, was getting in under the door. He was trying as hard as he could to keep the waves back. Everyone was there helping: Old Macaskill, Miss MacLennan, even his grandfather. Maria was nowhere to be seen now.

Suddenly there was terrible banging. Morag was trying to get in . . .

'Waken up, boy!' Waken up! We have to go and help Murdo!'

Michael woke up with a jump and knew the second he did so that it was twenty-five past three. His grandfather had been shaking his shoulder, perhaps for quite a time. The whole house was banging and jumping. He had never heard anything like it in all his life but he fell out of bed and found himself ready in his clothes. He was awake but he felt almost woolly, he way he did when he had 'flu, as if he wasn't quite there and everything took a little bit longer to understand. He wanted to ask about Murdo.

'The chimney's fallen down, Michael. We have to go and help get Murdo out. Your friend Fergus's father came to the door ten minutes ago. We have to take care going, d'you hear me?'

His grandfather was almost shouting in his ear. Michael nodded but that wasn't a lot of help in a dark room. But then a lantern appeared and he was walking behind his grandfather, going down the stairs with one hand on the banister. It felt just as if he was in a dream, in the same dream perhaps as the one he had wakened from. But there was Jess at the bottom of the stairs. Out in the street he was nearly knocked off his feet. There were people everywhere; there was calling and shouting, and at one point he heard the sound of breaking glass.

'Murdo's trapped! The chimney fell into his bedroom!'

He thought he recognised the person's voice but he wasn't sure. He tried to think and then he realised it didn't matter. His grandfather had shouted for him to come with

84

him and he was running behind him, his heart thumping. They got to Murdo's house at the end of the street. There were already three people there. Someone was trying the door to the left and it wasn't budging.

'Are you all right, Murdo?' he called.

There was a muffled answer from the other side.

'We're going to break down the door!'

'Be careful of my whisky!

They laughed at that in spite of the storm. Outside it sounded as though great booms of thunder were breaking over Coolin. Michael could hear the sea from there, roaring in over the walls and gardens. They counted to three and took a run at the door. It splintered. They ran at it again and this time Michael joined them. He closed his eyes as his shoulder hit the wood and he went on into the room with the rest of them as the door gave way. He hit the other wall and someone was patting his back; someone else was saying well done to him, and he could feel something sticky in one hand. They were trying to move all the bits of chimney from Murdo's floor.

'You should have knocked before you came in,' said Murdo. He had always had a great sense of humour, and even though he was ninety-four and the oldest person on Coolin, he was still as quick as anything with his replies.

'Can you put the chimney back where it was?' he asked the men who were clearing it up. 'I liked it better on the roof.'

In the end they all carried him on his mattress to Roddy's house. Even Michael helped. Murdo loved all the attention.

Round at Roddy's they all waited for a few minutes, talking about the storm. Michael was the youngest there. He didn't know why but it gave him a warm feeling in his tummy being there. He sat on a little stool close to Roddy's old stove, and Roddy's wife Jan gave him a cup of boiling hot tea that was dark as tar. The storm rattled against the windows like a furious robber trying to get in, but somehow he didn't feel frightened now. Suddenly Roddy put up his hand and seemed to hold his breath.

'It's lessening a bit, boys, you know,' he said softly.

'I wonder what it's been like out on the west,' said Michael's grandfather. 'They'll have had the worst of it, poor souls.'

'We'll soon see in the morning,' said Fergus's father grimly.

Michael found himself outside with his grandfather a few minutes later. The storm was getting less severe; it had changed now, and instead of one long thundering it was terrible gusts that came flying round corners and almost blew you off your feet. Michael heard the church bell striking four, very slowly and solemnly. There were people everywhere in the street; there were so many lanterns it was as though there were hundreds of fireflies.

'Did you know that Mary Ann lost all the slates from her roof?'

'Is there any news of Morag over at Claddich?'

'Mercy, me, and what's it been like up at the north end?'

'Have you heard the news, Dougal? Glasgow's fairly getting it!'

It was the strangest feeling being out in the street, in the very middle of the night. Everything was jet black because there were no street lights and the houses were all dark. The only thing Michael could just make out were the waves coming onto the shore. They were like great horses with flowing manes, crashing over and over with their white hooves on the Coolin shore.

Michael felt far away, even though there were so many people round him. Jenny appeared in front of him, thanking him for telling her earlier on about the coming storm, but he just nodded and half turned away. He was suddenly thinking about his mum and dad more than he'd done for a very long time. He had thought of his dad to do with the storm, but now he thought of them so hard it hurt. His mum used to sing a Gaelic song about Coolin, about the bit of water that lay between the island and the mainland. She used to sing it to him when he was frightened at night, and so he was sure he would never forget the sound of her voice as long as he lived. Why should he think of them so much now, he wondered? He couldn't begin to work it out. It was like waking sometimes in the morning and wondering why on earth you dreamed something. There was no reason for it at all. It just happened. He closed his eyes and leaned against the wall as the chattering went on all around him. He suddenly thought it sounded like knitting. All those words were like very fast knitting in the air.

But one by one the groups went off home. The skies were starting to get lighter, and the clouds were definitely beginning to break. Michael could just make out one or two of the far headlands. Everything was still different shades of inks, as if somebody had drawn the skies, the sea and the land with a very leaky pen. But there wasn't a single light anywhere. All the cottages and farms lay in darkness, and maybe it would be like that for days to come.

Suddenly he found his grandfather beside him. Michael smelled something familiar and he turned round in surprise to look at the old man. He had a pipe clamped between his teeth.

'You're smoking again!' he said in shock.

His grandfather nodded in the darkness and muttered into the pipe. He was looking away somewhere else. He sighed heavily and took the pipe out of his mouth.

'Fergus's father had an extra one. It's for my nerves.'

'If I find you another book from the library will you stop again?'

His grandfather chewed on the wood and there was a hissing as the tobacco glowed bright red. He was definitely thinking. 'If the book makes me laugh as much as *Three Men in a Boat*,' he agreed after a long time. 'Come on in, boy, I need my sleep even if you don't. We'll have a good strong cup of tea.'

When they went inside they found poor Jess hiding under one of the bookcases. Her eyes were black and mournful, and even though she thumped her tail in welcome when she heard their voices, she wouldn't budge. Michael's grandfather chuckled and got down on his knees and ruffled her black and white back.

'That's why they wouldn't have you as a sheep dog, isn't

it, Jess? As soon as anything frightening came along you were off! I know what'll tempt you out all the same, girl!'

The old man vanished to the kitchen. The house shuddered with a great gust of wind and Jess whimpered. Michael rubbed behind her ears, the thing she liked more than anything, but not even that took her mind off the storm.

Out of the kitchen came several slices of bread and the butter dish. There was something else there, though, that Michael hadn't seen for a very long time. It was a brass fork, about as long as his arm, and he remembered it was for toasting things. His grandfather took the grate off the fire.

'We may not have electricity, but we've a wonderful peat blaze. This is the way they cooked here on Coolin for hundreds of years! Come on, boy, you do the first one and let's see what happens!'

Michael speared the piece of bread on the fork and waved it over the glowing embers. It was almost too hot to hold his hand there. The bread began curling and he could smell it. So could someone else.

Out crept Jess from her hidey-hole, despite another gust of wind that rattled the old cottage. Her wet nose was searching for toast, the thing she loved most in the world. Michael and his grandfather laughed. They laughed happily together, but not just because Jess had come out for toast. They were happy, too, because the storm was passing and because Murdo was all right, because they were safe too. Jess ate her toast in less time than it takes to sneeze, and she seemed to have forgotten the storm already. Michael suddenly felt so good, so safe and content. He remembered that it was still the first day of the holidays. That was the best thing of all.

'Shall we go round and see how Morag is, boy? Tomorrow, I don't mean now, in the middle of the night.'

Michael nodded. He could show her the telescope. She would understand how proud he was of it. He yawned.

'It's bed for you, boy, or you won't be up till next Christmas, and the holidays will all be gone. Mind your step on the stairs in the dark and take a candle with you to bed. I'm going to have a last smoke here with Jess and then I'll be up.'

Michael suddenly wanted to give his grandfather a hug. He wanted to but he felt shy. Whenever he gave him a present his grandfather would always nod and shake his hand, and his grip was so strong it made you jump. He glanced back at his grandfather sitting in the old armchair with one hand on his pipe and the other on Jess's back, and suddenly he made up his mind. It was a bit like jumping into cold water. He strode over and put his arms round his neck. His grandfather smelled of tobacco and salt and Jess and Murdo's living room.

'Thank you for looking after me so well,' he murmured.

His grandfather made a funny noise that might have been words but wasn't. Michael got up to go and glanced back for a second. He was just looking into the orange light of the peat fire and his eyes were strange and shining.

11

A STONE had hit the window. He was sure of it.

Michael sat bolt upright in bed, wide awake. It was twenty five past seven in the morning and there wasn't a sound in the world. The storm had passed, almost as if it hadn't happened at all, and everything outside was completely and utterly quiet. But he knew he had wakened because a stone hit the window. He rolled out of bed and was dressed in a second. He opened his door and held his breath, listening. All he could hear now was his grandfather's soft snoring in the other room. Michael hadn't slept for more than three hours, but he felt very well rested just the same. That was weird. Normally when he got up for school after nine long hours of sleep he felt as if he needed at least another nine. Now there wasn't any school for six whole weeks.

He crept downstairs as quietly as he'd ever done before. The old wooden staircase was full of creaks and echoes, but he knew those stairs very well. It was as though he had a map of them in his head. He knew which end was best to put his weight on, and exactly how slowly. Then he was above a step he couldn't remember. Was it the middle part that was quietest or actually the loudest? He waited, thinking.

There was the sound of a sharp crack, and he looked up. He'd left his bedroom door open – that was another stone on the glass. George, Fergus and Ewan, he thought to himself – that was who it would be. But it was very early for them on the first day of the holidays. Michael decided it was the middle part of the stair and put down his left foot. The house was filled with a loud creaking, and he lifted his foot again as though he'd got an electric shock. He held his breath to listen for his grandfather's snore, but there was nothing. Now he could hear the old man turning round in bed; would he call out or would he get up to see what the noise had been? Michael waited and waited, not moving a muscle. Slowly the house went back to sleep, and finally he heard his grandfather's soft snoring once more. Everything was all right. This time he put his foot very gently at the left hand edge of the stair. It didn't make so much as the tiniest squeak.

That was him halfway. The rest he could remember, they were easier. He was down them in a few quick steps, and he hadn't made the slightest sound. He breathed a sigh of relief down at the bottom, outside the living room door. There was the tiniest sound from upstairs, from his room. A third stone against his window. If it wasn't all three of the boys then it was almost certainly Fergus on his own. Michael slipped out into the porch and put on his boots. Then he reached for the outer door and turned the handle.

'Maria!'

Of all the people he had imagined it might be, Maria was not one of them. Not after all this time and all that had happened.

She put her hand over her mouth to try to hide her laughter.

'You should see your hair, Michael MacGregor!'

He was completely bewildered. He would have been less surprised if the Queen herself had been standing on the doorstep.

She turned out into the street. 'Come on, are you coming to the north end?'

He didn't say anything but he did waken out of his trance. He closed the door securely behind him and was outside too. No-one on Coolin locked their front doors as they did on the mainland.

He saw her then over near the shore, laughing and making a fuss of Dawn the sheepdog. He started over, bringing his hand through his tousled black curls. What and how and why? He was completely bewildered. If he hadn't been so wide awake he would be sure the whole thing was a dream.

He just looked at her frowning as Dawn rolled on her back and had her ears made a fuss of. Then Maria saw he was there.

'I don't understand . . .' he began.

'Why I came? Why I came back?' She stood up tall and looked at him. His heart was thumping. They would be able to hear it over in Glasgow, he was sure of it.

'I didn't come back because of the lilies, that's for sure. Did you really think they would help, Michael? You said something that made me very upset, even though you didn't mean it. Flowers at the door just made me embarrassed!'

His face felt like a whole sunrise and he hung his head

and wanted the ground to swallow him up. Had she just come round to give him a row? Perhaps it was all he deserved.

She came a step nearer. She was close to him now. She'd be able to hear his heart for sure.

'I came because of what you said. When the girls were there, after school was over. I came because you cared. Flowers don't mean anything, they don't matter, but words do. Then I believed I could trust you.'

He dared to lift his eyes, just a little. But he still had no idea what to say. Whatever it was it was sure to be wrong.

'Come on, I'll race you to the north end. I bet I'll beat you.'

She didn't wait for him to answer. She was off up the road and it took him a second or two for him to think. Then he was after her. They took the shortcut through the village they'd gone that first time, on the day when they'd visited the cave and had talked about the Armada and treasure. The day that had ended so disastrously. . .

Now he was ten paces behind her and he wanted to catch her. He'd only slept for three hours but he was wide awake. He skidded on the gravel of the narrow path and she looked back to make sure he was all right. Then he remembered what she'd said. That it wasn't the lilies that had counted, it was his kindness. He felt a warmth in his heart at that. She had come back in the end, she had forgiven him after all!

Now Maria had turned the corner. Her hair was flying wild as she ran, and he thought of how often in the last weeks he'd hoped against hope she might turn round in her seat in the classroom and look at him. Now things might be all right again. Somehow that gave him extra strength, even though she had started ahead of him. He was maybe only eight paces behind her as they left the village and were up onto the straight road that led to the north end. They hadn't seen a single soul. Everyone was fast asleep, and even the sheep in the fields by the road looked strange, as if everything had been blown out of them.

There was a little hill ahead of them. The road turned round to the left and curled upwards before levelling off again for the last stretch to the north end. Somehow Maria wasn't quite so fast – was she tiring? This is where he had to do all he could to catch up, this was the best chance he had. She glanced out to the right, as if looking to see where he was, and he strained to speed up. His heart felt as though it was bursting as he climbed the slope, but he was gaining on her just the same – there were just two or three paces between them now.

He wasn't sure if he had any more in him when they came out onto the flat at the top of the rise. Now he could see Reneval and Skarva up to the north, that meant the beach would soon be in sight. The breeze was in their faces now, but it was just a baby compared with the hammering winds of the night before. Michael caught a glimpse of a bucket blown over in a field, then all at once he had a first sight of one of the dunes at the north end. Somehow knowing that spurred him on again, one last time. He closed his eyes and chased, and he felt Maria's elbow against his own as the two of them toppled over the first sand dune in a dead heat, gasping for breath and lying looking up at the sky.

Neither of them could move or say a word. He just felt happy that he had caught up with her. Not because he had wanted to beat her, not because he had wanted to win, but simply because it felt good. After all those months of wishing he could come back again with her, and thinking it would most likely never happen. He managed to open his eyes, and even that felt an effort.

Suddenly she was tugging at his arm and he glanced sideways. She was sitting upright, looking over the edge of the dune.

'Michael, look! Look what's happened to the hill!'

He didn't see at once; he wasn't sure what she was meaning. He leaned up on one elbow, frowning, looking past her towards the island's highest point that rose like a hunch-backed giant to lean out into the sea. Then he looked down into the water, to the bit round the side from his cave, from the cave they both knew. There were rocks in the water, large boulders that hadn't been there before. The edge of the hill, the steep side that went down into the sea – it had completely changed.

But Maria was already running down the dunes and onto the beach, heading over to find out what had happened. He called her name for her to wait, and either she didn't hear or wouldn't listen. He scrambled down after her, still tired after the sprint from the village, and limped after her as best he could. The wind had died all right, but the waves were coming in over the beach in great white combs, roaring and roaring.

When he got there she had passed the cave, gone further out towards those waves. He called to her to be careful but she was in no danger. She was scrabbling about far above the sea, in a rubble of rocks that hadn't been there before. They were sharp, and he went carefully, watching his hands and feet. What on earth had happened? Now she waited for him. She was watching him, her long hair billowing about her face in the tugging of the wind. He got there at last.

'It must have fallen down,' she said against the roar of the sea. 'The storm must have brought the rocks down, it was so strong.'

But he wasn't listening, he was pointing, his heart thudding. There in the wall that had opened up there was a gaping hole, a cave that disappeared back out of sight into darkness, into the hill.

12

THEY CROUCHED in the entrance of the cave, thinking. The waves shattered on the rocks below them and sent up great sheets of spray.

'Are we going or not?' she said, looking straight at him.

He wanted to but he was frightened as well. There were other caves on Coolin his grandfather had warned him about a hundred times before. There had been little dogs that ran in and came back days later with the hair all burned off their backs, and there had been bagpipers who had played until they were far in when the last notes of their tunes gurgled and disappeared for ever. Caves were not things to play with. He didn't answer but instead peered right inside, stuck his head into the low entrance.

'I can see something,' he said. His voice was muffled, as though he had his head stuck in a giant jar. He was sure there was something away ahead of him, something light. There was a flickering. He turned back to Maria who was still waiting for his answer.

'There's light inside, I'm sure of it,' he said, leaning back and looking at her. He was quiet for a second, still making up his mind.

'If we're careful. . .' He began. 'There's two of us. If anything happens, one of us can go back. And there's light in there. That makes all the difference. We can see where we're going, I'm sure of that.'

She nodded. 'All right then. You go first.' Her voice was quiet, but he could hear the edge of excitement in it all the same. She wanted to know just as much as he did. Something had happened after the storm, something had changed, and they were the first ones to find it.

'If there's any danger, anything that's not safe, we turn back,' he said. He remembered his grandfather suddenly when he had turned to go upstairs the night before, after the storm began in earnest. 'I need to come back for my grandfather,' he said softly.

She looked at him and her eyes glittered. 'And I need to get back for my dad.'

He nodded, understanding. Then he turned back to the cave entrance and put his hands on each side of the stone doorway, took his first step into the darkness. It was strange, that first moment when he crouched down and went inside. The roar of the sea suddenly changed; it wasn't gone completely, but it changed. It seemed further away and muffled, but the rocks all round him seemed full of noise. He crouched where he was inside and waited for Maria to join him, waited too for his eyes to get used to the dark. His grandfather had always told him he should eat his carrots so he could see in the dark – now he was thankful he had.

The cave was brightening with every passing second. He was on a kind of rock ledge, just as he had been out on the edge of the sea. Down below him was a channel of water, sea water. It came right into the cave, the cave that was much bigger than the little window he and Maria had climbed through. The channel of water was calm and deep. It went right on in under the hill, far further than he could see, and it went out into the open water of the sea. All round the outside, to Michael's right, were boulders that must have fallen down in the storm. This secret channel had been broken open by the sea the previous night.

Suddenly he remembered his walk up on top of the hill, not long after Morag gave him the gold coin. He'd been thinking about all the old stories of the ship inside the hill, and how none of them had made any sense. He had looked down at his feet and seen that flicker, and he hadn't known what it was. What if it had been the sea, that channel of water he was now looking at?

It went right under the hill, but until the night before it had been blocked and secret. It was only the storm that had opened it at last. Now that they were inside it was quite bright. He felt brave now.

'Shall we go on? It looks as though it goes deeper, quite a bit deeper.'

Maria nodded. It couldn't be that they turned back now, even though the inner part of the cave was shadowy, almost dark. They'd have to watch every footstep in case they slipped.

He started off once more and suddenly he felt something brush against his left hand. It was Maria's hand. He glanced back and met her eyes. She was holding his hand.

'Just for safety's sake,' she breathed, looking down.

He nodded and they went on, Michael leading the way. He used his other hand to steady himself because the boulders were so sharp and many of them unsteady. They were coming to a point of rock that jutted out into the channel. He had to find a way down and round, round into the last part of the cave, the bit that lay right under the highest point of the hill. The sea was further and further away. He suddenly realised it was warm. He looked up for a second and saw that the dome of the cave stretched into darkness. It was impossible to see the roof of it now.

'D'you think there are bats?' Maria whispered. 'I hate bats.'

He whispered back that he didn't think so, and suddenly wondered why it was they were whispering. He had to let go of her hand now, even though he didn't want to, so as to be able to work his way down to the bottom of the rocks and the edge of the water. He used both hands. It would be unthinkable now if one of them were to fall and break something. He tried to put the thought out of his head. They reached the bottom safely, stretched tall once more.

'What's that ahead of us, in the shadows? I can see something, Michael.' She pointed and he looked. He didn't say anything. It was too much to believe it was what he dreamed it might be. He didn't answer her, just started round the edge of the rocks and caught her hand in his own.

Now, it was easy walking, a kind of shingly beach. But with every step something grey was growing from the shadows, something amazing and beautiful. It was a ship.

It lay still on the water and it looked like a ghost ship in the half light. It had tall masts, and they reached right up into the cave under the hill. Now he could see the wood of the prow, and even in the half darkness he could see it shining. He was trembling all over because this was the greatest treasure he could have dreamed of finding. It was the Spanish galleon.

'D'you remember Miss MacLennan saying it couldn't be? That it was impossible?'

He could see Maria's smile. 'And my family, too. All the old stories that we had Spanish blood, from the time of the Armada!'

He laughed too and he felt so happy he could have sung and danced there under the shadows of the galleon. It was smaller than he had imagined it would be; quite a baby ship really. There was a ladder reaching down to the shore. He touched the wood, afraid it might crumble at his touch. But it was strong, just as firm as things his grandfather had made.

'I wonder what happened to them?' he breathed. 'To all the sailors?'

'They escaped,' she said at once. 'They left the ship and stayed on the island. That's what makes the old stories true. Then the rocks fell and blocked the cave entrance, leaving everything just the way it had been.'

He looked at her to ask if they should climb on board, but he knew he didn't need to. They had to go on.

Even so, he went very, very carefully. He tried to calm himself, to slow down. The sea flickered black and deep

under him. He reached out and stepped gently onto the deck, as if it was made of paper. An echo went through the whole of the cave. He turned round and stretched out his hand to help Maria aboard. They stood there together for a little, looking around them. Ahead of them was the open channel of water that led out to the sea. It got brighter and brighter the closer it got to the mouth of the cave. Above them the cave reached into darkness.

All at once Michael caught sight of the tiniest chink of light. Was it a fragment of sky? Then he thought of his walk that day. Perhaps that was the very place he had passed, the chink in the cave's ceiling. Behind them it was almost black. You couldn't see the end of the cave. Michael's heart drummed with joy. He had found the ship after all, and Maria had come with him.

'Shall we explore inside?' she said suddenly.

He nodded. There was a wooden hatch in the deck and they lifted it between them. It revealed an open square of darkness.

'On you go,' she giggled.

'Oh no, ladies first,' he said mock politely.

He did go ahead of her in the end and it wasn't as difficult as it had looked. There was a little ladder and he found himself down on a lower deck, dusty and dark. The air was somehow difficult to breathe. He wished he had brought a torch with him. There were tiny chambers almost too cramped to stand up in. There were what seemed to be little cannons and cannonballs, and tiny portholes looking out on the walls of the cave. They went everywhere blindly,

opening things and calling to each other and careful of every step. Then finally Michael kicked something and lost his balance, cried out as he fell. His hand was sticky. She helped him to his feet and he felt around, grumbling, for the thing that had tripped him. He found it, bent down to pick it up. It felt like a box, a little chest, and he could hardly lift it. They dragged it over to one side and he fought to open it. Now his hands were shaking badly. He could never have managed up the ladder. At last something broke and his fingernails found the edge of the lid. He opened it.

The two of them gasped. Even there in the darkness at the bottom of the Spanish galleon the gold coins glinted like candlelight. They ran their hands through them and the echo of their chinking filled the air and out into the cavern itself.

'I always hoped there would be diamonds and all sorts of jewels,' Maria said. 'I mean, I know this is treasure, but I thought of real chests like in Treasure Island.'

He could just make out the oval of her face in the grey shadows in front of him. He let the last coin fall back into its box.

'But you remember what Miss MacLennan said? She was right about one thing. They were warships, they'd never have come from Spain full of treasure. But you know, it's treasure all the same, I mean everything about it – the cave, the ship, this. To be the first ones to find it. Somehow that's even more than this box of coins. We'll always be the ones who discovered the ship in the end. After three hundred years.'

They carried the little chest back up onto deck between them. It was very awkward to carry, and when they were up they dumped it heavily down because of its weight and it tipped over, spilling edges of gold in every direction. The whole cave echoed with their ringing and clinking. Michael and Maria chased them across the deck and brought them back. They carefully poured them inside.

'I think that's all,' Maria said. He could see her clearly now. It seemed almost like broad daylight after the dark of the lower deck. Suddenly something came into his mind as he saw her carefully arranging the coins to close the lid. He remembered that day in the other cave all those months ago, and finally he had to ask her. 'Why were you so angry with me, that day when I asked about your mother?'

She looked at him and her eyes were filled with sadness.

'Because I didn't believe you cared. I thought you were making fun of me, the way some of the girls did. I thought you knew, that you knew as much as they did.'

He didn't say anything, just shook his head over and over again. He had known nothing, to this day he didn't know a single thing.

'My mum left my dad,' she said. She looked down at the deck below her and her long dark gold hair almost touched the wood. Even here he could see it glinting in the light from the sea.

'It was a long time ago and we still don't really know where she went.'

She looked up at him, her eyes glistening, as if she wanted to know what he thought. He dared to reach over and catch her hand. She had reached out for his in the first darkness of the cave.

'I wouldn't laugh at that,' he murmured. 'I lost my mum and dad.'

She looked up at him sharply, her eyes not understanding.

'I knew you lived with your grandfather, but I thought maybe your mum and dad were somewhere else. No-one ever said anything. . .'

'That's because no-one knows,' Michael said. He sat down properly on the hard deck, his knees hurting.

'I wasn't born on Coolin. That's something almost no-one knows. I mean older folk know, like Morag and Macaskill, but not people from the class. They think I was born on Coolin.'

'So where were you born?'

'Glasgow.' He half smiled in the shadowy light. 'I was born in Glasgow and my dad had a shop there. When I was three there was a fire. My mum and dad both died and I was saved. I was the only one that survived. My grandad brought me to Coolin.'

'Can you remember that?' she whispered.

'Coming to Coolin? Yes, just and no more. It was before the car ferry came. It was the old wooden boat, the small one. I can remember coming down to it and the smell of everything – the diesel and the salt water and the wood of the boat. I can remember being frightened by Old Macaskill's sheepdog!'

She wasn't sure whether to laugh but she did and so

did he. Their laughter echoed in that huge hall under the hill.

'We should get back,' she said, still keeping hold of his hand. 'They might be wondering where we are.'

He nodded, started to get up onto his feet, but she held him back.

'Thank you for not laughing,' she said softly. 'Forgive me for thinking you would. I was just frightened. You're not like the others.'

'Nor are you.'

They got up together and looked out at the bright water going out to the open sea. He knew he would remember that day forever.

'Shall we tell them about this, about the ship?' he asked.

She sighed and was quiet for a minute.

'I suppose we have to, but let's make sure we don't lose the ship, that it doesn't go to some museum in Edinburgh or Glasgow or London. It should stay here. This is where it belongs.'

He nodded. 'All right.' Then he suddenly thought aloud. 'We should get back. They'll be worrying about us. And this time we can't run!'

It wasn't easy with the little chest of coins. In the end Maria went down the ladder first, going backwards for safety's sake. Then Michael stretched down and handed her the box; he almost fell off the deck he had to bend so low. The box was so heavy that one of them would have to carry it alone; it would have been impossible to carry it between them.

Just as Michael's foot touched the bottom rung of the wooden ladder Maria gave a gasp. She had reached forward, was tracing her index finger along the wood. He couldn't see what it was in the shadows and he called to ask her. She turned and her face looked back at him like a pale moon. It was filled with happiness.

'The ship's name,' she breathed. 'It's the *Santa Maria*!'

Michael got down into the stones. He wasn't sure he understood.

'My name!' she hissed. 'Think about it! The sailors stayed after the ship was blown here, maybe in a storm, but they never forgot the name. And so when they married and had daughters they called one of them Maria. Remember I told you it was always said my family had Spanish blood, from the Armada? Well, girls were given the name Maria, to remember that. But no-one knew why it was Maria – my dad just thought it was because it was a common Spanish name. I'm sure it must have been because of the name of the ship!'

He thought about it too as they left the *Santa Maria* and struggled back through the rocks towards the little window they'd climbed through. It seemed to take an eternity and the box hurt his hands.

It was strange being back outside. The sun was gusty and the skies huge and blue; the two of them blinked like moles at first and their eyes stung because the light was so strong. They staggered about on the edge of the rocks until at last they were ready to move again. Michael's heart was beating hard. He was already thinking about the people he'd be able to tell: Morag, Miss MacLennan, his cousin in Glasgow who thought that Coolin was so dull and boring. His heart swelled with pride.

She laughed at him a bit carrying the box back home with him. He was all bent over, trying to keep a hold of it and walk at the same time, and when she made him look cross because she was laughing at him she laughed even more. He realised he must look a bit silly and the corners of his mouth began to curl with a smile too. The wind made his hair wild too; she said he looked like a haystack in a high wind.

'A very black haystack,' she admitted, coming close to him on the road that led back to the village. The wind blew her own hair across her cheeks and he realised how happy he was, how amazingly happy he was. He wanted this day to last for ever. He had hoped for so long that he would find a way to make her understand, and now he had.

'Will you come and say hello to my dad?' she asked.

He nodded. 'Of course. But will you take the box of coins the last of the way to my grandfather's?'

She nodded herself, puzzled.

'I have to get a book for him from the library,' he explained, 'or else he'll start smoking again.'

And he handed her the box and began running like the wind.

ᏰᎷᏰᎷ